IN THE ARMS OF THE RESTLESS SEA

A HEARTFRIENDS NOVELLA

CARRIE GESSNER

ISBN: 978-1-949665-11-6

Other Books by Carrie Gessner

The Heartfriends Epic Fantasy Series
The Dying of the Golden Day (#1)
The Shadow of the Endless Night (#2)

The Stroke of Thirteen
Empyrea and Other Stories

DEDICATION

This story is for:

My younger self, who longed for adventure

My current self, who still seeks purpose

And my older self, who will, hopefully,
continue to be guided by her heart

CONTENTS

ACKNOWLEDGMENTS

Writing books is a solitary pursuit, which usually suits me just fine. But there are many people who help me out and keep me sane during the process. In that vein, as always, thank you to my family for their continued support, and thank you to my community of writers.

I also want to thank everyone in my life who plays tabletop games with me. That might sound odd, but the pandemic has been tough mentally and physically for a lot of people, myself included. However, during this time, I started to play roleplaying games online and, when permitted, games in person. This has helped rekindle my love of storytelling and my love for the fantasy genre. So, thank you to all those people, who include (but may not be limited to): Chelsea, Christina, Erica, Erin, Heidi, Ian, Kathleen, Jason, Jeff, Joy, Matt, Meredith, and Tom.

PART 1

Nessa woke, but the world remained black. The acute pain in her head consumed her attention so that all she could do was mumble words of prayer to the Goddess to lessen her suffering. Long minutes passed before the ache receded enough to open her eyes. She was lying in the forest, and the early light of morning was peeking through the treetops.

"'Bout time," said a gruff, unfamiliar voice. "We can finally move."

Nessa looked around for the speaker, but moving her head too quickly sent another wave of pain through it. Keeping her breaths deep and slow, she lay her head back down on the scrub and lifted a hand to rub her pained, sweaty brow.

She paused. A rope bound her wrists together. Her mouth went dry as she scrambled to understand. The last thing she remembered was hanging the laundry to dry . . .

Rough hands gripped her arms and dragged her to her feet. The sudden shift made her vision blur. When it cleared, so, too, did the situation. All her sisters were here, all bound as she was. Ruya, Marie, Hilda,

Alyce, Kinnia, and the rest. Of them, she was the youngest by far—at least since Aurelia had left four years ago—and would be best suited to fighting back against their captors, two men and one woman. She recognized this part of the forest, which meant they weren't far from the temple. The woman and younger man were lashing Nessa and her fellow priestesses together by the waist. They would be marched to their destination, and with old women among them, their destination had to be relatively close. The less time it took them to reach it, the less time she'd have to think of a plan to save her sisters.

Oh, Goddess, she prayed, *be with us this day.*

"Let's go," growled the bigger man, the older one.

Sister Morran was at the front, and he clamped a hand on her elbow to get the line moving.

Nessa was at the end. Had they taken her last because she was the youngest or because she'd been outside? Or because she'd been the last to wake? Perhaps it didn't matter. Perhaps she was asking the wrong question. After all, the best way to know an enemy was to know their motivation.

"Why us?" she asked loudly, though the only sound was their footsteps and labored breathing. "What do you want with us?"

"Quiet!" bellowed the man in front.

A handful of the sisters winced at the anger in his voice, but neither of the other two captors reacted.

They trudged on. Nessa's skull was pounding again as if it'd been split in two. They had to have incapacitated her with a heavy blow. She checked for blood, but there was none on the front or sides of her head and she couldn't reach the back. The pain increased with each step, though, and now, she was nauseated and her hands were shaking.

A few minutes more, and the queasiness got so bad she had to fall to her knees, forcing the line to a halt. Tears filled her eyes as she retched. The bile burned her throat.

Sister Marie, the nearest to her in line, grasped her beneath the arms and heaved her upward, onto her knees. "Get up. You must get up," she said in a fierce whisper.

Nessa struggled to get her legs solidly beneath her. She wasn't fast enough.

The older man, the leader, grabbed her hair, wrenched upward, and growled, "On your feet. No more delay. And if you can't walk, you'll die."

She finally found her footing, though she swayed, and rubbed her sleeve over her face to soak up the tears and sweat and grime. It didn't matter, did it, what this man's motivations were? Anybody who kidnapped another person, took away their freedom, was acting against the Goddess and deserved to be punished. At least brought to justice. She couldn't punish him to the fullest at this very moment, but she could make his aim as difficult to achieve as possible.

She spat in his face.

Swearing, he lunged. She brought her arms up to protect her face while the man's companions rushed over to pull him away.

"Don't damage the goods," said the woman.

"This one's the youngest. She'll be worth the most," said the other.

The big man jerked out of their grasp and shoved her. "Back in line," he said before calling her a nasty name. As he walked to the front, he yelled, "Next one to give me trouble gets fed to the wolves. You understand?"

Nessa breathed deeply to calm her racing heart. Sister Marie threw a glance over her shoulder. The message was clear—if she angered him sufficiently, he might not stop at harming her. He might harm the rest of them, as well. Nessa wouldn't be able to bear that, so she ducked her head, swallowed her pride, and walked on.

It was nightfall before they reached the coast. She'd been wrong about how far they were being taken. The older women were weary, their movements slow and stuttered. Yet their captors dragged them on. Nessa fought against her instincts to shout and make a ruckus and give her sisters a respite. Unlike the others, her chest heaved with frustration rather than exhaustion. She felt powerless, but the Goddess would never lead her into a situation she couldn't get herself out of. Right?

All she needed was the opportunity.

Goddess, guide my steps.

With each footfall, she put her trust in the Goddess. Each time her boot struck the ground, she forced that thought into her head until the only word resounding through it was "freedom."

The land sloped downward, the grass becoming rocky ground. Inky clouds cut off what scant moonlight there was. Nessa kept her hands on Sister Marie's back to help steady her as they descended. Through the darkness, though, a modest boat was visible bobbing on the waves off the coast, and three smaller crafts lodged on the rocks. Where would they be taken? Slavery had been outlawed—if not outright, then in the forum of public opinion—nearly everywhere in the world. So, what was the purpose here?

Their captors let them pause as they consulted a ways apart, their heads together. Sister Alyce collapsed to her knees. As the others gathered around to help, Nessa's heart dropped. These women were old and exhausted. They'd not be able to fight back in the best of situations. By the Goddess, how was she going to get them out of this? Connected as they were, if she rushed their captors, she'd only drag the others into the fight. That meant she had to separate herself.

Crouching, she cast her gaze around for a sharp rock. None was as sharp as she wanted, but she didn't have the luxury of time. She chose a relatively long and narrow one, awkwardly maneuvered her hold on it to get it against the rope between her wrists, and sawed.

"You have to go," said Sister Marie.

Nessa whirled in surprise. "What?"

"If a chance should arise for you to escape, you must take it."

"I won't leave you, any of you."

"You must."

"What's this, now?" The smaller man snatched the rock from her grasp and flung it back to the ground. The clatter got lost in the noise of the surf. He cut the rope tying Nessa to Sister Marie and yanked her toward the last boat. "You're with me. Can't have you causing trouble for anyone else, can we?"

Nessa fixed him with a glare until his face paled and he gulped. He was afraid of her. He should be. Once they were in that boat, he'd be the only thing separating her from freedom.

As she stumbled in his wake, she glanced back at the other sisters, women she had known since she was a small child, women who had raised her and made her into the woman she was today.

A woman who could find strength even through her fear.

A woman who carried the legacy of an entire Order of priestesses in her bones.

"Goddess protect you, my child," Sister Marie shouted.

The others echoed it as their captors split them into two groups to load them in the boats.

Nessa's throat tightened. They'd traveled leagues. She'd had all day to think of a way to save them all, and now it was too late. The choice she now confronted was an impossible one—to stay with her sisters and face an unknown fate or to escape on her own with no home or safety to return to.

In the end, it was no choice at all.

I'm sorry, she mouthed, knowing they couldn't see it. This would likely be the last she saw of them, shadowy figures across a darkened stretch of coastline.

Her captor shoved her into the boat. She hit the wood hard, her head cracking against it and sending a flood of nausea over her. Her headache from earlier still raged. She leaned over the side to spit up bile, leaving her weak and shaking.

He wrenched her feet together and encircled them with rope. "Can't take any chances with you. There are a lot of things I'd do for money, but you're really starting to piss me off."

Nessa rallied herself. "How'd you get stuck with me, then? Short straw?" she asked, voice hoarse with pain. "The boss must not like you."

He looked indignant. "How d'you know I'm not the boss?"

She shrugged, or she tried to. Her body didn't seem inclined to listen. "I know a dull lackey when I see one."

"I ought to toss you overboard."

"Do it, then."

She slowed her breathing in an effort to regather her strength. They weren't even in the sea yet. She closed her eyes as he clambered out of the boat, shoved it into the water, and climbed back in. If they got her onto the ship, it would all be over. That meant the only escape route available was the surrounding sea.

This should have felt like a blessing, for water was her elemental gift, and yet there was such a chasm between making rain droplets dance on your fingertips and surviving a fall into the ocean with your limbs bound.

She gulped and thought of her sole and truest friend. Aurelia would tell her that it would be better to die free than to live confined. Then again, it was always easier for people outside of the problem to see the solution than it was for the person embroiled in it.

In that way and in many others, she and Aurelia had been helpmates to each other. And even though Aurelia was far away in the capital, she—or at least Nessa's memory of her—could still provide that help.

Nessa shifted so she wasn't quite as slumped on the boat's bottom. She took a few deep, rapid breaths in preparation for the plunge. Her captor, occupied as he was with his rowing duties, paid no attention to her. He seemed to want to get to the ship and be rid of her as soon as possible. Good. Let his preoccupation be her opportunity.

With one final prayer, she launched her body over the boat side. The water hit with a shock so great she had to consciously keep her breath in. Opening her eyes, she straightened her legs and let the water drag her down. When she was far enough down to be out of sight, she swam—as well as she could manage with rope around her wrists and ankles.

She didn't head for the coast. They would too easily catch up with her there. Instead, she chose west. With any luck, she'd be able to skirt far enough around the coast to get to a rocky outcropping out of sight where she could shed her bonds and make a run for it on land.

Her lungs burned for air, and the salt stung her eyes. She persisted nevertheless. She'd endure a little discomfort in order to escape. She reached for the power she held inside to assist her. Without any precedent for the magic she needed, it was a blind reach.

And, thank the Goddess, she managed to grasp onto something. The water surrounding her seemed to propel her forward as though it were carrying her like a babe in its arms.

Finally, when she could stand the pain no more, she broke the surface and dragged air into her lungs with great, gasping breaths. Shouting followed her. She dared not lose a second chancing a backward look, but the sound was far enough away to suggest her captors hadn't come after her. She shook the water from her face and, after one more breath, dove back beneath the surface.

With each flail, her muscles tired another tick. Worse—she could feel her magic weakening, too. Every pulse propel herself a shorter distance until she was barely moving forward at all.

When she ran out of air this time, she pushed for the surface, but she was too far beneath. She wouldn't make it in time. Her lungs were on fire. She stretched out her arms, hands still bound, reaching for the world above, for the air she desperately needed, as though it was not water but a mountain that offered finger holds to pull herself upward.

Her shoulders ached as she stretched. But she had to make it. She had to.

The tips of her fingers breached the surface just as the world went black.

The first thing Nessa registered was the fresh scent of the sea. Something plush cushioned her body from below. Without opening her eyes, she took stock of herself. The pain in her head had disappeared, though it would surely return were she to sit up. Her muscles, far from feeling overtaxed from her desperate swim, felt rested. Her lips were chapped, and her throat was dry, but she was, unexpectedly, alive. She opened her eyes to find a low rock ceiling hovering over her, and she sent up a small prayer.

If You see fit, perhaps I could stop nearly dying. For a fortnight at least.

A small voice cried out in excitement.

She wasn't alone.

Was it a child?

The language wasn't a familiar one. Did this person, whoever it was, mean her harm? Unlikely, considering she was still breathing. Though she wanted nothing more than to slip back into sleep until her body healed and though she barely had the strength to lift a hand, that wasn't how to stay alive. She braced herself for the pain and forced herself into a sitting position.

The ache came sharply enough that she sucked in air through her teeth. She squeezed her eyes shut, and when she opened them again, it had lessened. She felt for the wound at the back of her head, and her fingers came away coated in a sticky, dark green substance that smelled of algae. Confirmation, she hoped, that they meant her no harm, for they wouldn't try to keep her alive otherwise.

Relieved, she registered her surroundings. The cave was larger than she'd expected. There was no opening to a beach or any dry land. In fact, there were no openings at all. How did she get here? And who had brought her?

No sign of the person who'd spoken.

"Hello?" she called.

The only answer was the soft susurration of the water of the deep pool that lay before her. The surrounding cave, its walls glowing a gentle blue, was akin to the size of the temple in which she'd spent the majority of her life. A pang seized her chest. Would she ever return? There was no door or passage visible in the cave area, which meant the way out—if there was one and she wasn't trapped in some prison—must be through the pool.

Before she could decide on finding an exit or resting a while longer, a little girl popped out of the pool, a toothy grin on her face, water droplets glistening on her brown skin. As cute as the girl was, Nessa was taken aback by her sudden appearance. But at least it was confirmation that the passage was underwater.

"Hello," said the girl in accented but understandable Inantan.

"Hello," Nessa replied.

The girl swam to the edge of the pool and leaned her forearms on the rock. "My name's Freawyn."

"I'm Nessa. Are you the one who brought me here?" It seemed unlikely, but . . .

Freawyn shook her head. "That was Mama."

"Oh, right. Where is your mama now? And where are w—" The question died in her throat as a tail flapped lazily out of the water. Blue-green scales shimmered, casting flickers of light around the cave.

Oh. The girl had a *tail*.

Right. Yes. This made total sense. Mermaids weren't creatures found in legends and stories. Certainly not. They were flesh and blood, and the proof of it was standing right in front of her. *Swimming* right in front of her. Perhaps the blow to her head had done more damage than she'd realized at first.

"There's Mama! And Bryzo!" the girl shouted.

Two figures emerged from the depths of the pool. The adult must be Freawyn's mother, the young boy her brother.

Nessa felt light-headed. Aurelia, if she were here, would be losing her mind right now. Mermaids!

The merwoman put her hand on Nessa's chest. "Breathe, landbound. I imagine being below is a lot to take in."

Nessa gave a nod and endeavored to calm her breathing by inhaling slowly and deeply. After a moment, she said, "Below? Is this the ocean? Does that mean I'm . . ." She glanced at the ceiling of the cave.

"Under the surface of the ocean?" the merwoman asked. "Yes."

"Then how am I . . . How am I breathing?"

The merwoman gestured around the cave. "This is an air pocket. The anadulon growing on the walls aids in oxygen production, and mer magic facilitates our breathing as well as the breathing of those nearby. Even so, you won't be able to stay forever. Only until you recover."

Nessa nodded as tears burned at her eyes. She forced them away. What good would crying do? She focused on the merwoman's tail, swishing through the water. Her scales were a deep burgundy. The children, curious, attempted to approach, but their mother shooed them away until they were splashing and laughing at the far end of the pool.

"My name is Dima," the merwoman said, her voice gentle, as though regretting bringing up Nessa's imminent departure.

Nessa swallowed hard through a scratchy throat. "I'm Nessa."

"I'd like to examine your injuries now, Nessa, if that's all right."

With some difficulty and a gush of pain in her head, Nessa shifted and lay back on her elbows so Dima could inspect the wound on the back of her skull. Dima probed the paste there with warm, tender fingers and made small noises of concern.

"Does it hurt?"

"A bit," Nessa said.

"Where? What kind? Describe it for me."

"In my head. The back of it, but also the front."

"Constantly?"

"When I'm still, the ache is dull, but when I move, it's sharper. It's always there, though."

Dima's hands moved to her shoulders. "Any pain in your body?"

Nessa groaned at the touch. "Yes. Every inch of me hurts."

"Mm. You've been through an ordeal. You can't overcome that with a few hours of sleep."

Nessa licked her lips. Her throat was so dry. As if reading her thoughts, Dima swam to the narrow edge of the pool, plucked a glowing blue leaf from a vine, and held it under a trickle of water. When it was filled, she swam back and offered it to Nessa.

"Don't worry. It's fresh," she said.

Nessa closed her eyes as she drank deeply. The cool water soothed her throat. When the children saw what was going on, they brought her two more leaves, which she sipped slowly and with gratitude.

Once satiated, she asked, "You rescued me?"

Dima nodded.

Nessa bit her lip, hesitating. She should feel lucky that Dima had found her before it was too late. But what did she have left now? Even if she could return to the temple, there'd be no one to return to, and without the temple, what purpose did her life hold? Better that she had drowned.

"Why?" The word came out as a croak.

Dima's eyes, rich and brown, were concerned. "Sometimes," she said quietly, "we do not know how much strength we are capable of until the world shows us."

Nessa was anything but strong. She was small and wiry, and she'd always relied on Aurelia for support and companionship.

"Lady, are you sad?" asked Freawyn in her high-pitched child's voice. "Why are you sad? Would a story make you feel better? I can tell you a story!"

A smile tugged at Nessa's mouth. In a way, the little girl reminded her of Aurelia when they were younger. Freawyn seemed excitable while Aurelia had been serious, but Aurelia, too, had been interested in new things, new *people*. The realization only made Nessa's heart ache more for her old friend. Would they ever see one another again?

"Tomorrow," Dima said to her daughter. "Nessa must rest for tonight. Perhaps, if you ask politely, she will listen to you tell a story then."

Freawyn beamed at Nessa. "Can I? Can I come tomorrow and tell you a story?"

"You may," said Nessa, "but you must promise it'll be a good one."

"I promise!"

Nessa lay awake. By all accounts, it was night, but she wasn't sleeping. She couldn't. In the span of a day, her life had been destroyed, and she was left with the tatters. Only what was she supposed to do with them? She couldn't very well tie them together and weave them like a damn tapestry. Besides, she'd never been very good at needlework.

She ran a hand over her face. Without Dima and the kids to distract her, pain flared in her torso with every breath. It was slighter than it had been, but the twinge was keeping her from falling asleep just as much as the thoughts in her head were.

The few memories she had of her life before the temple were faint and scattered. Flashes of faces. A remnant of a voice. Even if she could remember her family, she had no names, no idea where to begin to look for them. The sisters had been her family. *Aurelia* had been her family.

Now, she had no one.

What was she without her temple, without her green robe of the priesthood, without her sisters?

She had always been a slip of a girl, thin and waifish. Far from strong and solid like Aurelia was. They had taken care of each other in different ways, and it was Aurelia's loss she felt most keenly. It was Aurelia's loss that summoned the grief she'd kept dormant until now. If her body didn't hurt so much, she would let herself cry. As it was, she allowed only a handful of tears before wiping the evidence of them from her cheeks.

Dima had said she couldn't stay here forever, which meant she didn't have long to plan. But what kind of life was there for her now? Even if she could find her way back to her home country, Sunniva was dangerous for people like her, and there was nothing left for her there anyway. Nor did she know anyone outside of Sunniva. There was no reason for anyone in the entire world to welcome her.

She had no one.

She had no one but herself.

That would have to be enough.

She had a few skills. She could read and write. Surely, that would be useful to somebody. And she could cook and do laundry and perform various domestic chores. Perhaps she could be a servant. Only if her master or mistress were kind, though. She didn't count her magic as a skill. A few tricks with water could hardly change her fate. Besides, there was no telling if other countries would treat the gifted as Temidorus did, with disdain and condemnation. No, she had to keep that side of herself secret if she could.

That settled at least part of it, and that would have to suffice for now. When Dima visited her again, she would ask which continent they were closest to. She could only hope it would be a welcoming one.

In the morning, after Dima had washed the wound on her head and reapplied the healing paste, Nessa felt well enough to sit up and partake of the food Freawyn and Bryzo had brought her. It consisted mostly of seaweed and underwater plants, and though the texture took some adjusting to, she felt better with sustenance in her belly. Dima looked on approvingly until Nessa ate the majority of what she was given before she departed for the day.

Nessa sat near the pool's edge with her legs crossed and asked Freawyn, "Well? Do you have a story for me?"

Freawyn nodded enthusiastically as Bryzo splashed in the background. "I have lots of stories! Which do you want to hear?"

"Hmm." Nessa put a finger to her chin as she thought. If her time with the merpeople was limited, what did she most wish to learn about them and from them? "Tell me about the ocean. Tell me about your home."

"We call her Nai Morunn. In your language, I think, that's Grandmother Sea."

"Oh, so, she watches over you?"

Freawyn nodded again. "She created us!"

"Grandmother Sea had all of the oceans to look after, and all the creatures relied on her," Bryzo added as he swam toward them. "She built them homes— reefs and plants and caves."

"But she soon realized she was lonely," Freawyn said.

Bryzo smacked the water in front of him. "I'm telling the story!"

"You weren't a moment ago!"

"Perhaps you can both tell me," Nessa interjected gently.

Immediately, the children's angry expressions faded.

"And the rivers and lakes where the landbound live are Grandmother Sea's sisters and kinswomen," Bryzo said.

"The landbound. Is that what I am?" Nessa asked.

"Yes!" they exclaimed together.

"Do your people interact with mine often?"

Bryzo folded his arms on the rock ledge and lay in the water horizontally, his tail flapping lazily. "You're the first landbound we've ever seen. Mama says we have to be careful."

"Careful of me?"

"No, she says you're not dangerous."

"But some of your kind are," said Freawyn.

That wasn't difficult to imagine, especially in light of how Temidorans had turned against people like her, people with the gift, so easily. Humans were nothing if not thirsty for conflict.

"Yes," Nessa said sadly. "I imagine some of us are."

"The queen wants us to stay away from the landbound, especially when we're little," Bryzo said.

"I'm not little," Freawyn complained.

"Yes, you are. We both are," Bryzo said in the tone of a child who comprehended more around him than he was given credit for. "When we're grown, we may join the scouting parties or minis— minist— ministerial groups like Mama says."

Nessa, still smiling at his stumble, asked, "There's a queen? What's she like?"

"She's Nai Morunn's representative," Freawyn said, "and it's her solemn duty to protect us. That's why she wants us to stay away from the land."

"Yes, that makes sense."

"She's very pretty."

"Is she? Queens tend to be very pretty, don't they?" With fondness, Nessa recalled the handful of times she'd met Queen Minerva of Sunniva, whom Aurelia looked up to. To hear Aurelia tell of it, the redheaded woman was as kind as she was beautiful. "What's her name?"

"Queen Fionshah," Bryzo said with a grin.

"Have you met her? Is she nice to you?"

"We've seen her loads of times," Freawyn said.

"At celebrations and such," Bryzo interjected.

"But we've only met her once."

"What else do you know about her?" Nessa asked, genuinely interested. The chatter took her mind off the pain, which, even though it had lessened, was still uncomfortable.

Freawyn looked at her brother. "What else do we know about her?"

"Um . . ." Bryzo tilted his head toward the ceiling as he thought. "She likes poetry!"

Nessa brightened. "Poetry? I adore poetry. Will you tell me some?"

Freawyn recited one in her native language, a lilting and flowing tongue, and Bryzo soon joined in until they were giggling.

Nessa giggled, too. "What does it mean?"

"It's about a naughty little eel who's too curious for his own good!" Freawyn said.

"Tell *us* a story now!" Bryzo demanded in that cajoling way children have.

"Hmm." Nessa tapped her chin, thinking. "Shall I tell you about Cadmon the Explorer, who was said to have a magic compass crafted for him by his beloved sister?"

The children's eyes lit up.

"We know Cadmon!" Bryzo said.

"You do?"

Aurelia had always liked the stories of his adventures and discoveries, and there were many, ending abruptly when his ship, *The Breath of the Naiad*, disappeared over a century ago.

"Yes! His ship is . . ." Bryzo made a face and looked at his sister. "Where's his ship, again?"

"Over in the eastern part of the sea," Freawyn answered.

"Do you know what happened to it? And to him?" Nessa asked.

"It got attacked by a kraken," Bryzo said.

"But it was an accident!" Freawyn insisted.

Nessa nodded. "Oh. Of course." Because of course kraken existed, too.

Astonishing. These children so casually held the supposed answer to a mystery that had plagued landbound like herself for a hundred years.

She leaned forward. "Tell me more."

And so they did, eagerly, until their mother came to collect them for supper, leaving Nessa to rest.

Dima took Nessa's hand between her own and turned it over to examine her palm. "Where does your power come from?"

"From my goddess."

"But in your body, where does it come from?"

Nessa flexed her fingers. It was true the sisters used their hands a lot when summoning magic, but she was never told where the power originated or if the movement truly helped. Perhaps it was all in their heads. It simply seemed natural. "I'm not sure. It seems to live inside me, and when I'm able to use it, using my hand to direct the energy seems to help." She shook her head. "But we know so little about our powers now. We used to know a lot more, but the teachings have been lost."

Dima looked up curiously. "Why is that?"

The dying of the gift was so ingrained in Nessa's life that she rarely stopped to think about it, but now, she recalled the teachings the elder sisters have given her. "With each generation, fewer children present with the gift. The last person known to have been born with it was sixteen years ago. We don't know why; that's just what happens. As for the knowledge, well, the older priestesses forget, scrolls mysteriously disappear without record, books get damaged, their writings unreadable. We're taught that it's the natural progression of things."

"Why, though? You said your gift comes from your goddess, yes?"

Nessa confirmed with a nod.

"Then why does she allow this . . . this wasting away?"

There were different theories, of course, but they all came down to one thing. "Perhaps we've angered Her somehow. Perhaps She's disappointed in us."

Humans carried so many sins on their backs. Would it even be possible to narrow those evils down until they discovered which was at fault?

Dima hummed, considering. "Perhaps, but what kind of goddess would not show you the way back?"

A chill seeped into Nessa's skin. This conversation was making her dwell too much on the future she always expected to have, the future that was now lost. It was reminding her that everything she'd trained for no longer mattered. "Some think She has."

"And you? What do you think?"

"I think if She has, She should stop being so damned obscure."

The pause that followed her words was soon split by Dima's laughter, sharp and loud and delighted. Nessa was so struck by it that she wondered whether the Goddess was here with them in this moment, trying to point something out to her.

"Do you think . . ." Nessa trailed off, shaking her head. The words had slipped out before her brain had caught up with them. No. It was silly.

"Yes?" Dima prompted.

Dima's gaze was friendly and inviting, and suddenly, Nessa wasn't so scared.

"Do you think I was sent here to learn from you? Just a little bit, I mean."

Dima or any of the merpeople didn't hold any secrets belonging to humans. They followed another path. But what if the Goddess had led Nessa here to retrieve a bit of knowledge that her people had lost and Dima's had retained? Perhaps it would be her duty to piece the Order's knowledge back together, bit by bit, country by country.

Dima shook her head. "Our peoples are so very different. Even if I knew how, it would take a lifetime. But you aren't meant to stay here."

Right. She was landbound. This world, however welcoming, wasn't hers.

But she no longer had a world to return to.

A few days later, when Dima insisted on discussing her departure, Nessa shook her head instinctively.

"I don't want to go home. I can't," she said, pulling her knees up to her chest.

Sunniva couldn't be home any longer, not if she wanted to survive, and all she wanted was to survive. Nearly drowning had taught her that.

"All right, all right." Dima placed a comforting hand on her shoulder. "Where do you want to go instead?"

The world was so vast, Nessa so small. How was she meant to make a decision like that? She might not even have the skills to handle life in a foreign land. But with Sunniva out of the question, she had to choose somewhere. Temidorus was too close to home, too hostile to her kind. Across the mountains, then. There was Raion, Lesu, Mydrost, all of whom had tense relations with her homeland. Those wouldn't do, either. To the south across the Sea of Velk, there was Krovol. The Krovolians were the ones who had invaded their land all those centuries ago, leading to Lucia uniting the thirteen clans. Although millennia had passed, she doubted they would look kindly upon her presence, and it held no enticement for her anyway.

It would have to be somewhere farther, then. Trallk, with its majestic mountains. Ulwendu, with its striking architecture. Or . . . or somewhere she wouldn't stick out so much, somewhere there were enough people of differing backgrounds that she could blend in.

Somewhere like the Western Isles, which were a smattering of islands populated by people from all over, travelers and merchants and pirates. If there were any place she could lie low and live anonymously, it would be there.

"Do you know the islands my people refer to as the Western Isles?" Nessa asked.

Dima nodded. "I will escort you there myself. Does that suit you?"

"You've already saved my life. An escort is too much to ask."

"Well, you did not ask. I offered," Dima said with a cheeky smile. The smile faded. "But tomorrow. We will go tomorrow."

The day and night had passed quickly, much too quickly for Nessa's liking. This wasn't her home, no, but it was tucked away from the world, away from the trauma she'd suffered at its hands. In a way, that had made her feel safe. The prospect of venturing beyond this cave brought a sickness to her stomach.

But perhaps she wouldn't have to be alone.

Goddess, she prayed, *guide my steps down the path You've laid for me.*

Goddess, grant me strength to face my trials.

Goddess, fill me with faith that I may live in service to You.

"You are frightened," Dima said.

"I am."

"You have to go."

"I know."

Dima's nod was slow and sad. "You'll never rest if you don't."

"I know."

Dima placed a palm on Nessa's cheek and kissed her forehead. "And so you have my blessing, landbound."

Nessa closed her eyes and breathed in Dima's cool scent, like the sea at dawn, as a golden warmth spread through her. "Thank you. For everything you've done."

"You will pass on my kindness one day," Dima said.

Nessa collected herself and wiped the tears from her cheeks.

"Come," said Bryzo, bobbing in the water and holding out his small hand. "We will be by your side. You won't have to be frightened."

She took it. "I'm scared."

"I know. But everyone feels fear. It's what we do with it that matters."

"Mama gave you a blessing," Freawyn said, taking Nessa's other hand. "That will give you strength."

Dima gave her one last encouraging nod and led the way through the pool and into a rocky tunnel. And Nessa, with her hands clasped in the children's, followed her out into the open ocean.

PART 2

Nessa went about her work, ignoring the shouting from the back of the shop. Idir, her boss, was a merchant and a relatively fair man. She rarely heard him bluster like this. But Randel was a special case. He'd come on as an apprentice six months prior, stellar references and all, but Idir had had almost nothing but muttered complaints about his attitude and his work since. Nessa suspected he was fudging numbers in order to slip more into his own pocket and using the excess to gamble at the taverns and gaming halls across the Western Isles.

Not that she was stupid enough to try to prove it. For now, for a long while to come, she had to keep her head down. That included keeping her gift hidden. One hint of it, and there was no telling who would run fastest to sell her out.

Her sisters hadn't sacrificed themselves a year ago for her to get captured again. For the sake of their memories, she would keep her head down.

So, she stayed focused on tending the shop. The mornings were particularly busy, and busy meant her head was clear. Anything to prevent her mind from settling on what haunted her in the quiet moments. By the midday lull, she had to venture into the storage room to unpack another box of sahhan, some of their fastest selling product. People liked it for its sweet taste that was combined with a hint of saltiness. On the weeks she did a particularly good job moving merchandise, Idir liked to give her a small bag as a reward.

Villosh was the first town she'd come to after arriving on the island of Tarroga. She'd intended on staying the night and choosing a destination in the morning, but she'd found she couldn't leave. As often as she was told there was more work, better work, in the inland fields, Villosh was along the coast, and she couldn't bring herself to leave the sea. The relentless surge of the waves called to her; she simply didn't yet know what it was saying.

If she put in effort, Idir might trust her enough that she would get to sail one day. Be a proper merchant's apprentice and travel to the other islands or even beyond in order to pick up and deliver goods. Though she'd find easier jobs elsewhere, she wasn't about to give up the possibility of the open ocean. The only way to get there, and she was determined to get there, was through proving herself as a reliable and hard worker.

And what then? Once she had a taste of the sea, would the life of a merchant be enough for her? Overnight trips once or twice a month and the rest of her life spent on the shore? If only Aurelia were here to consult with.

But Aurelia wasn't here. No one was.

Swallowing hard, Nessa gathered a dozen bags of sahhan in her arms, carried them to the shop floor, and stacked them in their proper place on the shelf. As always when she thought of Aurelia or the other priestesses—or even when she didn't—guilt and anger mingled and hummed through her veins. Because she'd done nothing to save them. Because she didn't know what to do for them now. If there even was anything to do.

A little voice whispered in her ear of revenge, as it'd been doing since that awful day. She shook her head, but it wouldn't dislodge. It never did. Instead, the forcefulness behind it increased with every move she made. Every product she put in its place on the shelf, every sum she added to a bill—it all was accompanied by *revenge*. She had a duty, right, to avenge the sisters who were taken from this world? She couldn't hide on Tarroga forever.

"Um, excuse me?"

Nessa whirled around. Her breath caught in her throat as her gaze landed on an unfamiliar woman. With her silky black hair tied in braids and high, pale cheekbones that looked like they could cut glass, she was more than simply unfamiliar. She was intriguing. Her looks spoke of Shanlin descent. Though the Isles were a hub of activity, they didn't see much traffic from Shanlin, far to the south and west, or any of the countries it bordered.

"Hi," the woman said, "I'm looking for soap. Can you show me where it is?"

Oh, even her voice was pretty.

So pretty it drove all thoughts of the shop out of Nessa's mind.

She blinked. "Um, uh . . . I don't think we have any."

"You . . . don't have soap?"

"No?"

"Is that a question?" the woman said with a smile.

"Uh . . ." Nessa gulped. Wait. *Did* they sell soap? That sounded familiar. Soap was a good, and they sold goods, so . . . it would stand to reason that it existed somewhere in the shop. But where? Never mind that she'd memorized the shelf and product arrangement by her second week in Idir's employ. It was as though all knowledge had vanished from her brain in the space of a moment.

No, she could answer a simple question. Her gaze flitted around the store. There in the corner—soap!

"Right . . . right this way," Nessa said, leading the woman to the appropriate area and gesturing to the shelves. "Sorry for the confusion. It's been a long day."

It hadn't.

"Here we have regular," she continued as she found some of her confidence again, "in addition to all manner of scents. Lavender, sandalwood, honey, roses, bread."

"Bread?"

"Bread-scented soap. It's actually quite popular." She pointed to a basket of creamy-white bars. "And this is goat's-milk soap. Made right here on the island. My favorite, actually."

"Is that so? Lots of options," the woman said, her gaze roaming over the shelves. "I came for boring old soap, so I'll take one of those. And a goat's milk for good measure." She picked up a bar of each and flashed a brilliant smile.

Nessa's own smile grew with each step—and she stumbled over her feet only once—as she led the woman to the counter to write up her bill.

"Have a lovely day," the woman said before walking out.

Words failed Nessa once again, but she managed a weak wave. Embarrassingly, she watched the woman's retreating form through the window until another customer snagged her attention to purchase incense from Raion and cloth from Lysend.

What a fool she was, losing her mind over a pretty girl. If Aurelia could see her now, she would be laughing so hard her face would turn red as a beet. But it wasn't Nessa's fault! She'd grown up in the temple with women old enough to be her mothers or grandmothers. And then there was Aurelia, her best friend. Even if she'd wanted to think of her in that way, they'd been young and consumed with other things.

Nessa simply didn't have any experience with . . . with whatever this was.

Despite the steady influx of customers, the rest of the day passed slowly.

At the end of the night, she made quick but tidy work of the day's ledger and locked it in its drawer. She slipped out the door and secured it behind her. A spring bite chilled the air, but having grown up in the colder clime of Sunniva, it was nothing she couldn't handle in her shirtsleeves. As she walked through town, it was easy to spot those who frequented the warmer areas of the world, bundled up in coats and even scarves. Before any of them realized, summer would slip in, accompanied by its steamy heat and the brilliant sun against the turquoise water. There wasn't anything like it in Sunniva.

She lived across town in a small, tidy room she rented from an old woman named Zinat who liked to feed her even when she wasn't hungry. It was pleasant to have someone who worried about her, but it wasn't home. It likely never would be.

It was a thought she couldn't stomach right now, so instead of walking back right away, she headed to the cliffs at the outskirts of Villosh. Nowhere near as high as the ones defending Soln Sert, the capital of Sunniva, which she'd seen only once, they managed to still remind her of home. Here, the wind teased her hair and her tunic. She inhaled an immense lungful of salty air, breathing so deeply it stung her nose and brought tears to her eyes.

Moonlight rippled off the inky swath that was the water below, the foam crests of the waves a palpable presence that threatened to drag down anyone who dared challenge them. The crash of the surf against the rocks reverberated through the night, steady, like a heartbeat. The more she listened, the stronger the call.

Was *that* where she was meant to be, out in that unending void? If it was, how would she know? She'd thought she was meant to be a priestess of the Order of the Most High Goddess, and look where that had landed her—on a strange island far away from anything and anyone she knew. If the Goddess had even laid a path for her, how was she to know if she was on it or if she had strayed from it? If she had strayed, how was she to find it again?

The questions were too big, too endless. They rang in her head until the ache wouldn't subside, and that ache only reminded her of the open wound in her heart. Ignoring that wound for over a year now had simply let it fester. Between the two of them, Aurelia had been the healer. Nessa didn't know where to begin with such a monumental task.

The pressure from the sound of the waves built in Nessa's ears and spread to her chest, so forceful she almost couldn't stand it.

Her boots went first. Then she stripped, leaving just her smallclothes. If the sea wanted her, the sea would get her. She backed a few steps away from the cliff's edge. She inhaled until no more air could fit inside her lungs and held that breath. As she let it out, she ran.

Another inhalation, and then a leap, and then she was past the edge, hovering over the watery abyss below.

She hung suspended—for a heartbeat, for a moment, for a lifetime. In that ephemeral forever, she was everything and nothing at the same time.

Then she plunged, her body breaking the surface like a boulder. The cold shocked through her as she sunk fast and far. Down and down, and the sound of the waves grew fainter. Or perhaps the pounding in her ears drowned out all else.

When her momentum slowed, she hovered. The salt stung her eyes, and the night was too black for her to see much at all. Between no sound and no sight, she felt almost . . . free. Letting her arms drift out to her sides, she floated there, a speck in the abyss. She was one tiny part of a much larger whole, but she felt it all. She was the ocean, and the ocean was her.

But soon enough, her lungs were near empty. Regretfully, she kicked her way to the surface, where the air tasted sweet and the water felt warmer now, as though nature itself were welcoming her with earnest arms.

Up above, the moon shone in a sliver, a silent sentinel. Were her sisters out there, looking at the same moon, or had they perished? For the first time since she'd left them, when she thought of her sisters, the thought wasn't accompanied by a longing for revenge. The pressure in her head dissipated, as did the tightness in her chest; the constant weight pressing down upon her shoulders was alleviated. She closed her eyes, tilted her head toward the moon, and, letting the salt of the water support her, reveled in a rare feeling of calm she couldn't find anywhere else.

"Thank you," she breathed out, though whether it was to herself or to the Goddess or to something else entirely, she couldn't say.

The winters in the Western Isles may have been milder than back in Sunniva, but the summers were another matter entirely. Even only two hours after sunrise, Nessa sweated through her thin tunic, vest, and breeches. That she was currently assisting Idir in unloading a shipment of goods didn't help. As Idir was busy with the paperwork, it left Nessa to do most of the actual lifting. Besides the heat, she didn't mind. Always wiry, she had been capable of her chores at the temple, but since coming to work for Idir, she'd grown strong. It made her proud that she'd become so capable.

The pride, though, was tainted with apprehension, because how was a life such as this in service to the Goddess? Sisters of the Order were meant to do good for others. The only thing she did all day was sell wares. Anyone could do that.

She cleared her mind by focusing on the crates she was shifting from the cart into the storeroom.

When she returned outside for another, Idir walked out of the main shop and sank onto a crate with a grunt. "I am growing old."

Nessa rolled her eyes at his bemoaning tone. "You're not old." He'd seen forty-five summers, at least, but just like her, the profession had kept his mind exercised and his body hale.

"But I will be soon." He sighed dramatically. "If only I had someone, someone I could trust, to take over my duties for me, act as my agent so I don't have to cross the seas so often, especially for the order from Tynthos next week."

She rested a foot on a box to catch her breath. "Going to Tynthos is hardly crossing the sea. There's even a bridge, so you don't have to get into a boat."

"Perhaps I won't have to get into a cart, either."

Right. Because *she* would be driving the cart.

Nessa turned slowly to face him. By the way his eyes twinkled, he seemed to think she would be pleased at the prospect.

She wasn't *not* pleased. But it was easier to let life happen to her instead of making actual informed decisions. A part of her heart resented Idir for forcing her into such a decision.

But it was a very tiny part.

"Nessa," he said with an air of unending patience, "you are too smart to continue this charade of a conversation, so let me simply ask you outright. Would you be willing to go to Tynthos in my stead? Just this once?"

"Just once?" There had to be a catch behind that.

"To see how you like it and to give an old man some rest."

Ah. "And once I return?"

"Once you return, it is your decision."

She lifted an eyebrow. "Do you promise?"

"If you absolutely hate it, I will never make you go on another trip again. But for what it's worth, *I* think you will make a magnificent trader. What do you say?"

She sighed. She *was* capable, and she was grateful to have the confidence of a man she admired, and perhaps it was time to stop hiding away from the world. Traveling to Tynthos would be a small but important step. If she did well, perhaps she could even go to kingdoms and lands that were farther flung, and perhaps that would calm the tempest within her, the one that called her to the sea in quiet moments of the night.

"Well?" he prompted.

"All right, old man," she said, "I'll go to Tynthos for you."

Idir beamed.

She smiled back without meaning to. She might even do him proud.

"An ale, please, Val," Nessa said, sliding into a seat at the bar.

Val, the proprietor of The Gulls' Rest tavern, filled a cup and placed it in front of her. "Heard you're leaving us."

"Where'd you hear that?"

"Idir, of course."

Nessa chuckled through her nose. "Only for a day or two. He's starting me small."

"Yeah, but you'll be out on the longer trips soon enough. And 'bout time, too."

Nessa sipped the ale, cool and refreshing. "What do you mean by that?"

"You know," Val said, shrugging, "just that I'm a bit surprised you've stuck around this long."

"Why's that?"

"You do my job for long enough, you see a lot of people come through your door. You start to recognize it."

"Recognize what?" Nessa had no idea what Val was going on about. Whatever it was, it didn't sound complimentary.

"That look in a person's eyes that marks them as wanderers," Val said.

Misonath. Child of the earth. Sister Ruya used to call Aurelia that. Nessa, too, occasionally.

"The one that says they haven't found their home yet," Val continued. "The one that says they might not ever find it."

Nessa gulped down half her tankard. "I've found a home here." The words sounded too defensive even to her own ears.

Val gave her a pitying look. She let Nessa finish off her ale before refilling it. "We've all got pasts, child. Sometimes they look like our futures, and sometimes they don't."

Val walked away to serve someone else, leaving Nessa alone with unpleasant thoughts she hadn't wanted to face. What was she meant to make of that? As far as she was concerned, the future didn't matter. All that was in her power was to live one day at a time.

Only the Goddess knew what the next day would bring, and it wasn't like Nessa was Her top priority.

She sipped her newly replenished drink and looked around. The tavern held both familiar and unfamiliar faces. Would *she* be one of those old familiar faces one day? Was she going to live out her days working for Idir and her nights drinking in this place? Would she even be happy doing that?

As she waded through those discomfiting thoughts, the tavern door opened and in walked a Shanlin woman. Nessa squinted until she recognized her as the one who'd come to Idir's shop months ago for soap, the one in front of whom she'd made a fool of herself.

Did the woman remember her? What if all she remembered was what a goose Nessa had been?

"Didn't your mother ever teach you it's rude to stare?" the woman teased, approaching the bar.

Sutkey. Nessa's face went hot as she turned back to her drink. "Sorry," she mumbled.

But then the woman plopped onto the stool beside Nessa, facing her, an elbow on the counter. "Well, did she?"

Nessa's gaze flickered to Val at the other end of the bar. She had no desire to incite her wrath by accidentally picking a brawl. Not that this woman looked the tavern-brawl sort.

"Didn't have a mother," Nessa said stupidly.

The woman raised an eyebrow.

"Well, obviously I had a mother. I never knew her. That's what I meant."

The stranger relaxed. "In that case, I'm halfway of a mind to forgive the slight, then."

Nessa chewed her lip. Best to smooth this over instead of letting it fester, and she never wanted to leave a pretty woman angry. "Would my purchasing your next drink make you all the way of a mind?"

The woman pretended to consider. "I believe it would, yes."

At Nessa's request, Val poured the woman another ale. Nessa raised her glass at the woman, who raised her own back.

The woman's smile grew. "My name's Min."

Nessa swallowed thickly and cleared her throat. "Nessa."

Min cocked her head. "I know you. From . . . from one of the shops in town, right?"

"That's right."

"So, have you been on Tarroga long?"

"Depends on what you mean by long. About a year and a half, a little less."

Min whistled low. "That would feel like an eternity to me."

"How do you mean?"

"It's just . . . I don't think I've spent more than a year anywhere. Other than Shanlin when I was growing up, of course."

So, she *was* from Shanlin.

"Left when I was seventeen and never looked back," Min continued.

"That's . . ." Nessa trailed off because she hadn't been much older than that when she'd been abducted.

When she'd escaped and left her sisters to years of hard labor or, worse, death. She wasn't much older *now*, really. Barely twenty.

She gulped her ale and used the warmth it filled her chest with to wash away the cold thoughts. She needed to loosen her death grip on revenge, but some days—the days when she was convinced she was doing all right and swimming along only to have the desire rear its head and consume her—were more of a struggle than others.

Min didn't seem to notice the dark turn of her thoughts. "It was my choice. I've never regretted it."

Lucky her, then.

"So, what brings you to Tarroga?" Nessa asked.

"I'm a navigator. My contract ended, and the captain was a bastard, so we, uh, well, we mutually parted ways."

"Is that what you're doing here, looking for work?"

Min nodded. "Figured the Isles were as good a place as any."

As a mere merchant's apprentice, Nessa couldn't really help with that. She didn't know anything about sailing, and Idir was only trusting her with a cart, not a ship.

They talked through their drinks and ordered another round.

The intensity of her curiosity was embarrassing, but Nessa couldn't help it. She could count the number of people she regularly conversed with on one hand, and beyond that, Min was fascinating. "What's it like? Shanlin?"

Min hummed, and the pleasure in her eyes at reminiscing over her homeland was delightful. "Green. Lush. Sometimes when I think about it, I can still smell the cherry trees."

"That sounds lovely."

"Which has you wondering why I left."

Nessa dipped her gaze, focusing instead on running her thumbnail back and forth on the rim of the tankard. "You don't have to tell me."

"Perhaps I will one day," Min said. "Besides, I could ask the same of you."

Inhaling, Nessa straightened on the stool. "How do you know I'm not from here?"

Though descendants of the original inhabitants of the Isles tended to have browner skin than Inantans, centuries of the islands being used as centers of trade and commerce meant there was no longer one way for an Islander to look.

"It's the eyes," said Min. "Travelers can always tell their own kind."

Why did people keep saying that to her tonight? Nessa sipped her ale again. Her head was starting to feel fuzzy. At the rate she was going, using her drink to give herself time to think, she'd have a raging headache in the morning.

If people could tell her heart was restless simply by looking at her, what else could they tell? That she harbored a darkness she couldn't shake? All this festering guilt from not being able to save her sisters?

Min's eyes sparkled. "I told you where I grew up. Now, it's your turn."

Clearly, she thought they were kindred spirits, both travelers following their wanderlust. She didn't know that Nessa was as much a prisoner as she ever had been. Instead of temple walls—which, no matter how comfortable and protective, had still been a type of cage—the thing that kept her stuck in place now was her own indecision. She was hemmed in by the sea and by herself.

"Sunniva," Nessa said flatly. No point in lying; no point in telling the truth.

"I've never been, actually. How did you like it?"

Nessa bit her lip. Why did she feel seconds away from sobbing? She blew out a long breath until the feeling receded. "I don't know. It's all I ever knew."

"Until now."

"Until now," Nessa said.

There was a beat of silence. She was beginning to draw into herself, as she did with Idir and others when they got too close. This woman was practically a stranger. She didn't owe Min her life's story.

"Well, Sunniva isn't that far, much closer than Shanlin," Min said with a chuckle. "You can go back as often as you wish."

"Except I don't," Nessa said, her voice harder than she meant. But she didn't apologize. Instead, she drank the rest of her ale in three big gulps and set the tankard on the counter with a clatter. "There's nothing left there for me."

It was midafternoon by the time Nessa reached the bridge spanning the nominal distance between Tarroga and Tynthos. Gunther was Idir's finest horse, an import from Trallk. His breed were big, burly, and could pull huge amounts of weight without complaint. Their load on this trip wouldn't be overly heavy, at least half of it the firestones that Tynthos was rich in. The breed was also gentle, and Gunther was a breeze to handle. He seemed to know where she was going better than she did. Perhaps that was true.

The bridge was a wide thing built of wood and split by a rail down the middle so those traveling north could pass on one side and those traveling south on the other, to keep traffic moving. The bridge spanned a dark, choppy sea. The wind had kicked up this morning, making the water even rougher.

She brought Gunther to a halt as a boy of perhaps fifteen or sixteen jumped down from a squat tower at the side of the bridge.

He sauntered up to her. "Halt there, miss. What's your business on Tynthos?"

"Trade," she responded, retrieving her medallion on its cord from beneath her tunic and holding it out for inspection. Idir's mark, a series of intersecting lines that resembled his initials, was stamped into it to show she traded on his behalf.

"What sort?" At her hesitation, the boy said, "Textiles? Gems? Coin? Metal goods? Weapons? Religious artifacts?"

"Coins in exchange for gems, produce, and miscellany."

He nodded sharply. "And when are looking to come back?"

"Late tonight, but tomorrow if necessary."

"All right, then." He made a few marks in his notebook, tore out a paper, and handed it to her. "Show this to the bridgeman on the other side."

"Thank you."

She made to urge Gunther onward, but the guard held up a hand.

"You should stay the night, travel back tomorrow."

"Why?" she asked with a quirk of an eyebrow. The nights came late in the summer, and even so, bridge certainly seemed sturdy enough to pass over in the dark.

"I'll be off for the day in an hour, but I'll be working tomorrow." By the cock of his head, he seemed pleased with himself.

"Oh . . . Thank you for the information." The entirely useless information. Why in the otherealm would he think she needed to know that?

With a curt nod, she urged Gunther onward. He walked up the bridge ramp with a leisurely step. She endeavored to match his ease during the short crossing.

The bridge worker on the Tynthos coast greeted Nessa with a nod. "Can I direct you anywhere in particular, friend?"

Idir had given her directions to her destination. Wouldn't hurt to reinforce them in her head, though.

"I'm headed to a trader's. Name of Occu."

"Right. Go straight on through town. Turn left at the apothecary."

"Many thanks."

She clicked her tongue to get Gunther moving. The sun had reached its zenith but was still high in its descent. If Occu wasn't too busy, she could make decent time and be back on Tarroga by nightfall. Not that she had anything waiting for her there.

She smoothed her hair down in the breeze as Gunther led them through town. She felt settled, to an extent, in Villosh. So, why did she feel so restless now?

She shook her shoulders and shook the brooding thoughts out of her head. She didn't have time for that. She had a job to do.

Once she made the left after the apothecary, it was only a few minutes more before she arrived at Occu's. The trader's was a two-story building made of hard, weathered wood. A balcony jutted from the top floor. Far from the bustling outpost she'd expected, this seemed near abandoned. Even the structure was dilapidated, shored up with newer boards, nailed haphazardly into place.

Nessa jumped off Gunther and tied his reins to a nearby post. "Hello?" she called. "Occu?"

No answer greeted her.

Well, she couldn't wait around forever.

The door opened with a light push. The inside was much different—and much improved—from the outside. Wares like toys and supplies and weapons were organized by category and neatly displayed on tables and shelves. Display cases held the largest assortment of fancy gemstones and jewelry that Nessa had ever seen. Strange for a place with such expensive goods to be so unprotected.

Or seemingly unprotected. Perhaps she had walked directly into a trap. She forced the tension that had appeared at that thought out of her shoulders. Idir always said she was on guard with the world when she didn't need to be. It was true. Besides, this was a trading post. People who ran trading posts had no reason to set traps for unsuspecting new merchants.

"Hello?" she called out again.

This time, she did get an answer.

"We're closed! Come back tomorrow." The voice came from a back room whose door didn't even come up to Nessa's shoulders.

She stepped toward it but didn't try to open it. "I work for Idir on Tarroga. He said you'd be expecting me."

A muffled sigh was followed by a clang, as though the person within the room had set down a tool with unnecessary force. Footsteps. Then the door opened a crack—seemingly on its own.

But no, the man who opened it was simply very short, about the height of Nessa's waist. It didn't help that he peeked out barely an eyeball.

She pulled the letter from her pocket. "Details of the order. From Idir."

The man didn't even glance at the letter she held, instead rolling his eyes. "Occu's out for the day. Some kind of emergency. She'll be back tomorrow."

"Can't you help me?" she asked. "Since I'm here now?"

"I make things. I don't sell them."

Nessa tamped down her irritation. What kind of trader left in the middle of the day and didn't leave behind someone who could manage the shop?

But badgering the man wouldn't do any good. Idir didn't expect her to return until the next day anyway, no doubt hoping she'd take the evening to explore and have fun. As though she even knew what fun was.

No matter. She'd find the nearest inn, order supper, and find a book to while away the evening.

"Fine," she said. "I'll be here with the sun."

The man sent her off with a scowl.

Well. That was pleasant. Goddess willed that Occu would be here to meet her on the morrow.

The Foam Crest Inn was a decent-looking place, with one big room with a central fire and a doorway that presumably led to the kitchen. It was warm and dry, and it would do. Nessa found an open table in the corner with a view of the entire room. Being able to see those who entered and exited set her more at ease. No one paid her any mind. She was an outsider in these Isles, as were many people. It was easy to disappear in a place such as this—a string of small islands under the crown of no kingdom.

The barmistress, Helda, brought her an ale, and she ordered a meal. She kept her palm wrapped around the tankard as she sat in silence, her gaze sliding in and out.

She was a stranger here—fitting, since she felt like a stranger to herself. She'd let so much time go by telling herself that survival needed to be her first and only thought. The Order taught that everyone needed a purpose in order to fully live, but survival wasn't a purpose, and her stability in Villosh meant she was long past the point where it needed to be her single, solitary goal.

So, what was she waiting for? Life had taken her from the temple walls, and she had forgotten all that she'd been taught. Shame churned in her gut—at herself and her failure.

She gulped the ale, and as she brought the tankard down, her gaze caught on a table across the room. A woman and a man sat there, but it was the woman who commanded Nessa's attention. She wore breeches and knee-high boots, and brown curls spilled out from beneath her hat. Her long, double-breasted coat was thrown open, revealing a white tunic, the laces loosened. With one foot resting on the chair beside her, she looked the picture of ease and arrogance. Nessa envied her that.

Then the man said something to the woman, and the woman glanced over, a smug grin on her striking face. Nessa looked away, but she couldn't escape the feeling that she'd been somehow caught.

Minutes later, it became clear that she had.

The barmistress approached her table and set down a fresh cup of ale.

"I'm not finished with this one yet," Nessa said.

Helda tilted her head in the stranger's direction. "From the one over there."

At Nessa's uneasy glance, the woman raised her glass. And she winked. The haughty bastard.

Nessa looked down at the table. "Do you know her? Them?"

"In passing. She's a captain—ruthless but respected as far as I've heard—and he's first mate. Her crew come in occasionally, too. They alternate their shore leave among the different islands." She regarded Nessa curiously. "You have an interest in pirates?"

"Pirates?" Oh.

Helda chuckled. "Ah, you didn't know."

"No," Nessa said with an embarrassed chuckle.

"Haven't seen much of the world, then, have you?"

It was a strange realization—especially after having been abducted from her homeland, finding herself stranded in the ocean, and starting a new life, or something like it. But truly, there was so much out there she knew nothing about.

"No," she admitted. "No, I guess not."

"Well," Helda said kindly, "the Western Isles are a good place to start."

Nessa sank into her chair as the innkeeper walked away. When she lifted her gaze again, she found the pirate captain staring at her with a smirk. Nessa broke the stare to sip her ale, and the woman chose that moment to stand and stride in her direction.

Goddess, what could she want? And what was it about this woman that so vexed Nessa? She didn't want to cause any trouble, especially not the kind of trouble a gifted could find herself in, but this woman had apparently taken an interest in her.

Accordingly, she swung the chair across from Nessa around, sat on it backwards, and leaned her arms on the chair back. And she stared.

Until Nessa shifted uncomfortably and asked, "Can I help you, friend?"

"Don't know yet," the pirate replied. "What's your name?"

"I'm not in the habit of giving it to strangers." Nessa's fingers tightened around her tankard. No, she wasn't looking for trouble, but neither did she want to chat.

"Then how do you ever meet anyone?" The woman's sea-blue eyes sparkled, and she reached out a hand. "I'm Sabeen. Will you tell me yours now?"

After a brief hesitation, Nessa shook the proffered hand. "Nessa."

Sabeen's smile was a lot softer than she'd expected. "Nessa. That's beautiful."

Nessa had no response to that. No one had ever said anything like it. Her cheeks grew warm, and she wished she could will the blush away.

"Come join my friend, Ekvar, and me at the table," Sabeen said, indicating Ekvar with a tip of her chin.

Nessa sipped, tapped one finger on the table. "Why are you so interested in me?"

"I find you . . . curious."

"Oh, yeah? And why's that?"

"There's a look in your eyes that I recognize."

Nessa twisted her lips. Impossible.

But was that her fault? Because she refused to let anyone in? With her only friend out of reach, there was no one she'd even allow past her walls.

"You don't know me," she said quietly. "Nobody knows me."

Sabeen rose, turned the chair around, and pushed it in slowly. Expression sorrowful, she said, "Perhaps not. But I did know your father. Quite well, in fact."

And she walked away.

Nessa sat stunned for a moment, the words not quite registering.

What . . . What had she meant by that? Was it even possible? *Nessa* didn't know who her own father had been. How would this strange woman she'd never met before know?

Perhaps it was a trap. But to what end? Nessa had nothing to give . . . except her gift. Was Sabeen the pirate actually a bounty hunter, luring her into a trap to finish what the others had started?

Her knee jiggled, her boot heel tapping against the wooden flooring.

Or . . . was this a sign from the Goddess? A sign to knock her out of complacency and make her *move* instead of waiting for the wind to take her where it willed?

She gulped down the rest of her ale in three big swigs. Then she pushed out of her chair and strode to Sabeen's table.

"What are you talking about?" she demanded. "No lies. Do not lie to me." She couldn't take being lied to, even by a stranger, not about this.

The two pirates exchanged a heavy glance. Did the other one—Ekvar, Sabeen had called him—had he known her father, too?

Sabeen held out a hand toward an empty chair. "Have a seat, Nessa."

"No," Nessa said, jerking her arm away from Sabeen. "Tell me what's going on. I need to know. I *deserve* to know."

"Sit down, Nessa," Sabeen said patiently. "There's a lot to tell. We'll need another round of drinks, and your meal should be just about ready. Sit, and we will talk this through."

Nessa was not typically an angry person—perhaps because of spending much of her youth wrangling Aurelia. At least, she hadn't been an angry person before the abduction. Now, her hands were balled into fists that shook with the rage she'd locked away for the past year. Why was it that everyone seemed able to affect her life except herself?

"Please," Sabeen said, voice and expression pleading.

It snapped the tension in Nessa's shoulders. She reached for the center of calm the sisters had always taught her to cultivate, and she sat.

Ekvar gave her a kind smile. "You'll feel better when you have some food in you, too."

"Yes, we'll wait for Helda to bring your supper," agreed Sabeen.

Nessa studied Sabeen's face for any hint of a lie. Not that that was a skill she'd acquired in a temple of priestesses who tended to be honest to a fault. Despite her lack of practice in reading people and her penchant for distrusting them, something tugged at her heart.

Pay attention, it said.

More than that, there was something familiar about the shape of Sabeen's eyes, the curve of her nose, the arch of her brow, so familiar it made Nessa feel like she had known her in another life.

But that was impossible.

Helda brought out a meal of soup and flat bread rolled and stuffed with rice, meat, and vegetables. After thanking the barmistress, Nessa took a big bite. It was hearty, and spices exploded on her tongue. By the time she'd eaten half the food, her stomach was filling and her unease was disappearing. Strange how doing something as simple as eating could calm one down.

Finally strong enough to hear what Sabeen had to say, she started on the soup and looked up.

Sabeen nodded sagely, seeming to understand. "You look just like him, you know. My brother."

Nessa's heart clenched, and she set her spoon in her soup bowl. Of everything she'd expected, she hadn't expected *that*. In all her twenty years, she'd barely given her parents a thought, never imagined which one she more closely resembled. If she looked so much like her father, then her father could have been a lost twenty-year-old in a new tavern on a strange island once, too. Perhaps he was out there still.

She took a long, slow breath. A myriad of questions swam through her head. Until she finally processed Sabeen's words.

"Wait. Your brother? So, you're my..."

"Aunt, yes."

"What . . . What was his name?"

Sabeen's breath hitched. "Right. I forgot. You were so small when we took you to the sisters. You wouldn't have remembered." She put her hand on Nessa's forearm and gave a slight squeeze. "His name was Maxim."

Maxim. Her *father*. Having been given to the temple when she was a mere one year old, she had no memory of him. What was he like?

"And my mother? Did you know her, too?" she asked.

"Yes. Helena," Sabeen said.

Helena. She closed her eyes and tried to conjure a face, but nothing came. Still, hearing their names made them real. They had been flesh and blood, they had been people with dreams and plans, and they had given her up for her own good as well as the good of their land, their traditions. Had they dreamed of having a child, raising her, only to sacrifice her in the name of the Goddess?

"You're certainly? Absolutely certain?" Nessa asked.

"I asked your name because I wanted to be sure," Sabeen said. "But even if you'd changed your name, I would have known. You look *so* much like him. When I saw you sitting over in the corner there, it was almost like I was seeing him when we were much younger. He had a mustache by your age, though, I think."

Despite feeling as though she'd completely lost her footing, even while sitting, Nessa chuckled. She turned to Ekvar. "You knew them, too?"

He nodded. "Not as well, but yes. Your father, mostly."

Nessa took a spoonful of soup. Though it was a warm day, she was suddenly chilled from the inside out. "Were they . . . like you?" She couldn't bring herself to name the profession, not at this moment, when her parents were realer than they'd ever been to her before.

Ekvar smirked, but it was a gentle expression, wistful, like he was recalling fond memories.

"No," Sabeen said. "Not even *I* was like me when you were born."

"So . . ."

"Maxim was a baron in Temidorus, like our father before him. His wife became baroness. They had you, and . . ." She hesitated, her thumbnail running over a gouge in the table. "They were well-off and well respected, and when they found out you had the gift, they had no choice but to give you up. I assure you— it was the last thing they wanted."

"I understand."

And Nessa did. It was the way of things in Sunniva. Or Temidorus, since that was apparently where she was from. It was a fact of life, not something to get upset over. And by the sounds of it . . .

"Is he alive?" She licked her lips. "Maxim?" She couldn't bring herself to say the words *my father*. They seemed so foreign.

"No," Sabeen said quietly. "He died a handful of years after you went to a temple."

Oh. She wouldn't have gotten much time with him anyway.

"And Helena?"

"Became baroness and continued her duty. As far as I know, she's still alive, but we drifted apart. The Purge changed things."

When King Aras outlawed the gift from Temidorus. Of course that would have changed things.

"Is that how you became . . ." Nessa began cautiously. "I mean, if you were the daughter of a baron, then how did you . . ."

"Turn to piracy?" Sabeen smirked. "That's a very long story. One for another time, I think. But anything else you wish to ask you may."

Nessa frowned. Questions tumbled around in her mind, so many vying for attention that it took her time to recognize which one was claiming the most.

"What's it like?" she asked. "Being on the sea?"

Sabeen tilted her head. Her eyes bore into Nessa's, and Nessa shifted uncomfortably. Had she said something wrong?

Sabeen leaned close and dropped her voice. "You feel it, don't you?"

Her gaze flitted between Nessa's eyes, as though she were trying to reach deep inside her to claw out the secrets she held close.

"The call of the open sea," Sabeen clarified.

Nessa gulped her ale. Her element was water, and hadn't she, deep down, felt the truth of that? Every time she stood on the docks gazing out at the waves. When Dima and the merpeople had nursed her back to health in the underwater cave. The ocean was a part of her, as though it were in her bloodstream.

Did that mean anything, or was it a lucky guess based on what Sabeen wanted? Based on what Sabeen wanted Nessa to be? How was she to know what she wanted if people kept expecting things of her?

This woman had known her father, but she didn't know Nessa. No one knew her, not like Aurelia had, and until she grew the courage to return to Sunniva, Aurelia was lost to her now.

"And you're here to, what, get me to join you?" she asked.

Sabeen cocked her head. "I'm not here *for* anything, love. Fate pushed us together, which I happen to think is worth celebrating."

Brows creased, Nessa shook her head. This was too much all at once. She needed a break, she needed some air, she needed things she could neither articulate nor identify.

She pushed back from the table. "Thank you for the meal."

"Nessa." Sabeen grasped her wrist, the hold unthreatening, light enough to be easily broken. "We leave at midday tomorrow. *The Winged Lady*. Come find me beforehand if you wish."

Nessa acknowledged the offer with a curt nod before rushing out of the tavern. It was all too much for her, everything she'd learned tonight, and a building with four walls and a ceiling couldn't hope to contain such feelings. Only the sky and the sea were vast enough to cast her worries into.

As it turned out, Occu was a tall, charming woman. Reddish brown hair tumbled down her back, and she wore a complicated outfit of bright fabrics. Her gauzy outer layer—Nessa couldn't quite call it a coat—swished around her calves as she bustled around the shop, helping customers and merchants.

"Ah, yes," Occu said as Nessa stepped toward the counter. "You're Idir's apprentice, are you not?"

"That's right." Nessa presented the order for Idir's items.

Occu scanned it. "Excellent. Shouldn't be but ten minutes. Why don't you take a look around while you wait?" And she disappeared through a doorway.

Nessa wandered around the shop. Though she hadn't drunk much the previous night, her head hurt now, made worse by the heat of the morning and the fact that she was sweating through her clothing. She tugged at the collar of her tunic to cool herself down as she glanced over the wares, which looked to be from all over, from Mydrost to Zheyr to Krovol to Zadai. Perhaps one day, she'd visit all those places and more.

The weapons section in particular caught her eye. She'd never needed one at the temple, where the sisters lived peacefully. That hadn't protected them, hadn't kept them from becoming a target. Not that being trained in defense would have made a difference.

But she was alone now. The only person she could rely upon for her protection was herself.

A shiny dagger on a shelf drew her eye. Its blade was the length of her forearm and looked freshly sharpened and oiled. The faceted handle was crafted from a black metal she didn't recognize, with small words she couldn't read etched into it. No firestones or other jewels encrusted its hilt. Compared to the other daggers for sale, this one was plain.

She plucked it off the shelf with her fingertips and rotated it in the sunlight streaming through the nearest window. As she did, the gold filigree in the etchings became clear. The words weren't one of the handful of languages she knew by sight. They could be anything.

She curled her fingers around the handle to test the dagger's weight and balance, like she'd seen those who'd come into Idir's shop do. Despite the angles, the handle felt comfortable, perfect for her hand, as though it molded itself into her palm. It felt . . . right. And nothing had felt right in a very long time.

"Ah, an excellent choice," Occu said from behind her. "Made from the purest obducidean in Zheyr."

Nessa quickly replaced the dagger on its holder. She wasn't embarrassed, only caught off-guard.

"Not to worry! They're on the shelves to be sold." Occu picked it up and admired it. "These types of weapons used to be much more sought-after, but they've been out of fashion for decades now. I can let it go for a song."

"Let me guess," Nessa said, settling into the role of a merchant's apprentice. "A special price just for me."

Occu's grin showed large white teeth. "Oh, I like you. I bet Idir does, too. Not a special price, a fair one."

The price she named was, indeed, a fair one. Low for a dagger even, but as she'd said, ones like this weren't in demand. And though she had no training in wielding it, it felt so right in her hand that she couldn't bear to leave without it.

Once she bid Occu goodbye, with the goods loaded up into the cart and paid for and a new blade at her hip, it was time to return to Tarroga and to Villosh. Her job here was done.

There was only one more thing she wanted to do.

The small harbor on the southern tip of Tynthos bustled, still hectic this late in the morning. Sailors, merchants, dock workers, and yes, even pirates, shouted greetings to each other or sang as they went about their tasks.

Familiar with the atmosphere of an island port, Nessa found what she was looking for quickly. *The Winged Lady*, a handsome galleon, floated alongside the far pier. It was an imposing but sleek vessel, and she had no doubt it boasted more speed than any other specimen here.

She walked up the gangplank onto a busy deck, pirates going to and fro as they readied the ship. Despite the crowd, it took her no time at all to locate Sabeen, who was instructing a younger mariner on proper knot-tying or something. That stupid hat.

"Nessa," Sabeen said when she caught sight of her. She smiled widely. "I'm glad you came. It's good to see you on a ship."

"I didn't . . . I'm not here for long." She wasn't here to join them is what she meant.

"Fine," Sabeen said. Her smile dropped, but she wasn't angry. "What is it you need, then?"

Nessa squinted off into the gently roiling water. Try as she might, she still couldn't scrub the desire for revenge from her heart. That was why she was here. Was this woman—her aunt—someone who knew that feeling?

"Information."

"About?"

Nessa hesitated. "Have you ever crossed paths with bounty hunters?"

Sabee's shoulders tensed. "What do you want with bounty hunters?"

The Western Isles were a fusion of people. It made it easy to blend in, easy to hide. That was probably why pirates liked them so much. But surely people who hid well could find others who didn't always want to be found.

"Still distrusting, are we?" Sabeen said, though she didn't sound impatient. "Here's a better question." She let Nessa's anticipation grow as she knotted the rope she was holding. "What have they done to you? If you tell us, it will be easier to identify who it was."

"Does it matter?" Idir had been right when he said she guarded her privacy as though it were gold. He had also been right when he said she'd never get anywhere with an attitude like that.

"Unfortunately, yes." Sabeen's voice was stern. "You see, there are two types of bounty hunters. There are the decent ones, the ones who go about their business with the right papers and don't make more trouble than they need to."

"And the other ones?" Nessa asked.

"They're the scum of the earth, lower even than the men who live and die by greed and power."

Nessa tried not to let her surprise show. Pirates thought bounty hunters weren't worth spitting on?

Obviously it did show.

"We have a code of honor," Sabeen said, affronted. "Just because it differs from most people's doesn't mean we don't have one."

Nessa scuffed the toe of her boot against the ship's planking to buy time to turn that over in her mind. "So, these scum bounty hunters, you would say they include the ones who have abducted the gifted—say, sisters of the Order of the Most High Goddess?"

"Ah. And sold them into slavery, yes."

"Slavery?" Nessa's heart dropped.

"Those are the rumors, at least. They were targeting gifted. Still are, too, just doing it quiet-like. Biding their time between jobs, striking when people think the threat is over again. It's nasty work."

"Then you know who they are? Their names, where they operate."

Sabeen took her off to the side, away from the others, and, voice deadly serious, asked, "What is it you want, Nessa?"

The question taunted her. It had been since she was taken from the temple.

Revenge, her heart whispered. She tamped it down, Dima's words ringing in her ears. She was a priestess of the Order of the Most High Goddess. She was supposed to be above petty things like vengeance.

But what if she wasn't?

"Nessa. Tell me the truth. If it's revenge you're after, that's a long and difficult road, and it's one that will destroy you."

Nessa met Sabeen's fierce gaze with an equally fierce one. "I just need their names. Then I'll be on my way."

"No."

Nessa blinked. "Wh-what?"

"I won't give them to you."

Nessa turned away. "Then where's Ekvar? Perhaps he will."

"By the Cho've, you're just like your father."

Sabeen laughed ruefully, but when Nessa turned, her expression was bittersweet. She burned to know what Sabeen meant but was too proud to ask. She burned to know about her father. And her mother.

But there was something worse that she burned for more.

Sabeen rested her hand on the hilt of her cutlass, fingers tapping in agitation. "Revenge won't heal you. Trust me—I know."

"I'm not looking for it to heal me."

What did she want then, for it to destroy her? Perhaps destruction was preferable to this half-life she was living, where nothing truly mattered. Where she didn't allow anything to truly matter.

Sabeen's gaze drifted to the newly purchased dagger on Nessa's belt and back up. Her tone was bitter when she said, "If you listen to one thing I say, only one, let it be this. If you do not heal, this desire will consume you, like a festering wound. In seeking to annihilate your enemy, you will instead annihilate yourself. You will wake up one day not knowing yourself, and you will not like who you've become."

The steel in Sabeen's eyes made Nessa falter back a step. She sounded like she knew from experience.

It seemed the only two choices were to seek revenge—even if it ruined her mind and her soul—or to let the pain of her failure—to protect those who cared for her, to make something of her life, to follow in the Goddess's footsteps—ruin her.

"You cannot go on as you are," Sabeen said, softer.

"And how is that?"

"Lonely."

Nessa took another step backward.

"Nessa." Sabeen grasped her arm.

Nessa pulled it away. Then she walked down the gangplank with a tear rolling down her cheek.

What the otherealm was she supposed to do now? Nessa stood on the pier, hands curled around the railing as she stared out at the blue-gray sea and the ships docked for the evening and felt the salty wind on her face. Every day for three weeks now, she had thought of her mother and father. It had never bothered her before, the fact they had left her with the Order as soon as a sign of her powers was known. That was simply the way it was. Aurelia's story was much the same—and those of all the sisters before them. She and Aurelia had grown up with a dozen mothers, some kinder than the others, so it truly hadn't mattered.

And yet, ever since Sabeen had given them names, had said Nessa resembled her father, her parents had become real people, not memories or figments. How was she supposed to move through life as though she were still the same person she'd been before she knew that? It didn't make sense. Nothing made sense.

Nothing except the tranquility she felt when on the water. Standing here now, she felt the pull again. Perhaps Sabeen had been right and she did belong on the sea—*to* the sea. In that case, she'd fallen into a fine profession even if merchanting wouldn't have been her first choice. How odd the concept of choice was to a former priestess, anyway.

She dropped her head into her hands. Her mind felt like a tangle of roots. When trying to separate one thought, the rest came with it, and each one complicated the ones that came before.

"Idir said I might find you here."

Nessa picked up her head to find Min leaning against the pier railing a few steps away. Min had asked after her?

"He said you're down here almost every night."

"I like the water. I find it peaceful," Nessa said.

"I haven't seen you at the Gull in a while."

Nessa dropped her gaze back to the water. "I've been . . . busy."

"I've heard. Settling in as a proper apprentice?"

"Something like that."

Min came closer, her head tilted. "You've been out of sorts. Do you want to talk about it?"

Did she, or did she want to keep it inside until she could stand it no longer? Her instinct was the latter. She fought against it. Because here was Min, open and sweet, wanting to know about all the bad things that had formed Nessa. Goddess knew why.

And perhaps, in the depths of her heart, she knew Sabeen was right. She knew she couldn't last much longer, not like this.

"It's hard to explain," she said finally.

"When people say that," Min said, "I find it usually means they don't know how to talk about it. It seems easier, safer, to hold onto things. And it is in the moment. The problem is that down the road, it usually gets to be too much, and then . . ." She made an explosion noise and spread her hands apart, fingers wide. "Oh, that's trouble."

Indignation flashed through Nessa at the implication until she realized what was happening. She straightened at the sight of Min's smirk. "You're trying to get me to talk about it, aren't you?"

"I'm doing nothing of the sort," Min protested, but her expression said otherwise.

Nessa couldn't hold back the laugh that bubbled up. It'd been so long since someone had teased her, since she'd felt comfortable *being* teased. "Fine."

Min nodded, waiting patiently for Nessa to gather her thoughts, which was neither an easy nor a quick task.

Eventually, she said, "I was a priestess back in Sunniva."

Min gently tilted her head. The tip of her tongue poked through her lips as she thought. "Inantans worship a goddess, right?"

"Yes, the Most High Goddess."

"That's what you call her?"

"Mm-hmm."

"Oh. Our gods have better names."

It drew another chuckle from Nessa, which, by the look on Min's face, was the reaction she'd been after.

"Why did you leave?" Min asked.

"I didn't. Not by choice." She looked down at the rippling water, like she could see the faces of her sisters there. There was so much more to say, but the words were caught in her throat.

After a moment, Min rested her hand on Nessa's forearm. Nessa exhaled, and it felt like the first exhalation in over a year. It was the reassurance in the touch more than anything that gave her the courage to, for the first time, tell the story. Quiet and concerned, Min listened. That, too, helped the words come easier.

When she was done, Nessa wasn't certain if they'd been standing here for five minutes or five hours. No matter how much time had passed, she was a different person. Fundamentally. From her inner core outward.

Min gathered her into a warm hug. Goddess, it had been *years* since anyone hugged her. Not since Aurelia. Nessa closed her eyes and sank into it.

"You've been through a lot," Min said when they pulled apart. "But you've made it so far, and I'm glad you're here today."

The warmth in Nessa's chest spread to her cheeks.

"I bet you think about them a lot," Min said.

"All the time." Nessa hesitated. "They gave themselves up to help me get free, and now all I want to do is avenge them."

"Ah. And you want to know if I think you're a bad person."

"No. Yes. Perhaps." Nessa ran a hand over her hair. As with any time someone asked that, she didn't know what she wanted.

Min changed tactics. "What does your goddess say about killing?"

"That it's reprehensible, of course."

"In all circumstances?"

Well, no. *The Book of the Goddess* and the other texts were full of nuance. The Goddess's attitude toward revenge, though, *that* was clear.

She brushed off the thought. "What does it matter? I'm not a priestess anymore."

"It matters because you may not wear the robes of your Order, you may not live in the temple, but the Order is who you are. They raised you, formed you. You can't simply let go of that."

Nessa let that simmer in her mind. The temple and its sisters had taught her to seek goodness and to spread it. Yet her heart was so bent on the opposite right now. How was she to reconcile that?

"Let's say you did find out who these bounty hunters were," Min said patiently. "What then?"

"What do you mean?"

"Say you find out their names, where they were, all of that, and you went to them. What would you do to them?"

Nessa was young, but she was no longer naïve. If she delivered the vengeance her heart cried out for, she knew it would be hard. It would be the hardest and worst and most damning thing she would ever do. And yet . . . she'd still try.

"I'd want to kill them," she admitted.

"But would you do it?" Min asked. "Knowing that would go against everything you knew as a priestess?"

"That's what Sabeen said. That I'd regret it. That it would destroy me."

Min hummed thoughtfully. "And do you think that's why you're so angry with her? Because she told you what you already know in your heart to be true?"

Nessa cursed under her breath. She'd been so blinded by anger. How many times had the sisters warned her against anger when she was growing up? Not even two years out of the temple, and she'd forgotten all her lessons, all their teachings.

But why couldn't she push this wicked thought from her head? Was she not a good enough person? Would she struggle with this compulsion the rest of her life? If so, she couldn't bear it. Aurelia could have shouldered this burden, but not Nessa. She wasn't strong enough.

Groaning, she closed her eyes and pressed her fingers into them and bowed her head. She wouldn't cry, not here in front of Min, not now.

Min placed a solid palm between her shoulder blades, a grounding touch.

"But how do I overcome it?" Nessa asked, lifting her head. "How do I move forward?"

"I don't know," Min said softly. "But I think wanting to move forward is a good place to start, and I think we can figure it out together."

Following a long day in the shop, Nessa walked into The Gulls' Rest and immediately spotted Min at a table near the back.

"Hey," Min greeted her, pushing a tankard toward her. "Got you a drink."

"Thanks. I'll get food?"

Min acquiesced with a nod.

At the bar, Nessa leaned on her elbows as she waited for Val to finish with another customer. They had been doing this more often over the past few weeks. Perhaps it was the routine or the food or the friendship, but it brought her comfort, and Goddess knew she needed that.

"Evening, Nessa," Val said, sauntering over. "Meals to go with those drinks?"

"Please."

"Bring 'em over in a minute," Val said. "Oh. Letter for you, by the way." She produced it from beneath the bar before disappearing into the kitchen.

Nessa looked at it with a frown. There was her name right on the front. Not that she thought Val was mistaken, but who would be writing to her? Outside of customers, Idir and Min were pretty much the only people she interacted with.

Nessa glanced over at Min, who gave a cheery smile. She returned it with a soft one of her own and then opened the letter.

My dear niece,

I feel we left things unsatisfactorily, and I find I cannot let it stand. I hope you will do me the honor of reading this through even if you're still upset with me.

I imagine you are. Sometimes family are the easiest people to be upset with.

Know at the least that I say what I do because I care about you. I always have—from the moment you were born to the moment you were sent away. And then again to the fateful night I saw you again, when the Goddess surely guided us back to each other. Believe me when I say I thought of you every day in between. Your father did, too, until he died. I hope that brings what comfort it can.

I understand you've been through an ordeal, even if I don't know details. Perhaps I never will. And perhaps this advice is as worthless as the word of a good-for-nothing king, but I wouldn't be a proper aunt if I didn't at least try to tell you.

Here it is: I've seen revenge and its aftermath. It always seems worth it until it isn't. The fires of vengeance consume everything, including yourself.

Take that for what you will, but I'm not in the habit of skirting the truth.

If you've read this far, you have my gratitude. My offer to sail with us stands, and it will until I've taken my last breath. The Winged Lady *will dock in Villosh on the fourth day of Kalcetryn until the following morning. I'll be at the docks during that time should you wish to join the crew or merely say hello.*

And if you never receive this, or if you burn it without even breaking the seal, then the Goddess shall know that my love and goodwill go with you.

Your devoted aunt,
Captain Sabeen Mathan

Nessa folded the letter with a shaky sigh.

Sutkey.

Nessa was an easy person to leave and once left, an easy person to forget about. Every time the sisters sent her on a chore as a child, she'd had the feeling they forgot her existence as soon as she left a room. Even Aurelia, with her good heart, hadn't been able to prevent it. Prior to Nessa's leave-taking from the temple, Aurelia's duties to the prince had been growing with every season, and her letters had been coming less frequently.

Then there was Sabeen. She was blood, whatever that meant. It meant something to her, it seemed. And despite their brief encounters, despite the tension they'd stumbled upon, she had made the effort to reach out. To explain herself.

To offer, not necessarily an apology, but a hand.

"Bad news?" Val asked, interrupting her thoughts.

Nessa came out of her head. "Uh, no, not exactly."

Val only nodded. The question had been polite, not probing.

Tapping the edge of the letter on the bar top, Nessa waited another minute for Val to hand over two plates of food from the kitchen and took them over to the table, saving the barmistress the trouble.

"You all right?" Min asked, already shoving a fried potato wedge into her mouth.

Nessa wasn't *not* all right. What she *was* was confused. In a warm way, if that made any sense at all. It was hard to explain, and she didn't think she could put it into words for Min. Instead, she pushed the letter across the table.

Min waited for Nessa's confirmation nod before opening and reading. Nessa, who had given her a barebones explanation once she'd returned from that fateful trip to Tynthos, couldn't seem to stop jiggling her knee as Min read, her eyebrows rising with each line.

Finally, Min folded the letter and set it down. "Wow."

"Exactly," Nessa said.

"Are you going to go?"

"I don't know. I feel like I don't know anything anymore." Did anyone, really, when it came down to it? The world was colossal; people were mere specks of dust.

"Hmm."

Nessa turned to her meal, a hearty dish with creamy rice and fish. Food was never a bad choice. When in doubt, eat a meal. That was what old Sister Alyce used to say.

"What would you do if you were back in the temple?" Min asked through a mouthful of potato.

What she'd always done. "I'd pray about it," Nessa said.

"So, that's what you should do. Go pray."

"There's no temple nearby." Nessa had never seen one, but she still didn't know the Western Isles well.

Min waved her fingers dismissively. "Is your goddess bound by temples, though? You always talk about her influence being all around you."

Nessa frowned as her words came back to bite her. That was true. The Goddess was everywhere. But the temple was about ritual. It was about quieting your mind so you could hear Her. Never the most dedicated priestess, she'd always needed that aspect more than the older, more experienced sisters.

"I bet you can find somewhere that makes you feel like the temple did," Min said.

The temple offered more than quiet. It offered peace, both of the body and of the mind. What sort of place here offered her the same?

Suddenly, it didn't seem so difficult. Being too inside her own head kept her from realizing the solution. It kept her from remembering something else important, too, something she'd gotten out of the habit of.

"There's a prayer we say often, whenever we're walking or eating or working or simply thinking."

Much like being in a temple, the purpose of reciting the prayer was to help center oneself.

"What's the prayer?"

Nessa looked down. "Goddess, guide my steps down the path You've laid for me. Goddess, grant me strength to face my trials. Goddess, fill me with faith that I may live in service to You."

"It's simple," Min said.

"Oh." Nessa deflated ever so slightly.

"Simple and lovely."

"Oh." She wasn't sure why Min's implicit approval meant so much to her. Perhaps all it meant was that

Min was a safe person with whom to discuss the matters close to her heart.

Min made sure to catch Nessa's gaze before saying, "It seems like you have a plan."

"I do?"

"You're going to find a place that makes you feel calm—maybe the docks in the evening; you like the water—and you'll recite your prayer as many times as you need to to find clarity."

Somehow, when Min said it, everything seemed so easy.

"Yeah," Nessa said thoughtfully. "Yeah, I can do that."

"Good." Min smiled. "And then whatever you decide, I'll be by your side. If you want me. I could use a good adventure."

A week before Sabeen and *The Winged Lady* made port in Villosh, Nessa closed the shop for the night and walked down to the sea. She took her time, and with every other step, she had to convince herself not to go find Min at The Gulls' Rest. This was something she had to do on her own.

Lamps lighted the streets; the walk through town was pleasant in the cooling evening air. Storefronts and stalls were closing down for the day, their proprietors preparing to go home for supper or stop by a tavern first. Normal people going about their normal lives. Even if she did settle here, would she ever be a part of that? Or would she always long for something else, something . . . more?

Her usual path took her down to the water and to the docks, but tonight, she wound her way past the final pier to where the bank was grassy enough to not be very desirable as a beach. With the latening hour, too, she had this area all to herself.

Good. Otherwise, she wouldn't have the courage.

She kicked out of her boots, stripped down to her underclothes, and strode out into the sea. The dropping temperature was already leaching the day's heat from the water, but she didn't flinch at the chilliness. She barely even noticed it. She kept her gaze on the horizon, kept her breathing even and slow, and kept her mind clear.

When she made it out far enough that the waves reached her waist, she plunged in. For what she had to do, she couldn't be this close to shore. She had to feel like all that surrounded her was ocean and more ocean. By the time she reached that, the sun had disappeared completely and stars poked out of the firmament one by one, wink by wink.

Exhausted, she floated on her back, giving herself to the gentle motion of the waves. Her arms floated out to her sides, fingers curled up ever so slightly toward the sky, waiting.

To give or to take?

Above, the moon was in a crescent, waxing, and from this angle, it looked almost like a spectral smile. Perhaps it was watching over her.

If she put this off any longer, the sun would rise before she made her decision. She only hoped the Goddess was listening.

Three deep breaths to center herself, and then she said, "Goddess, guide my steps down the path You've laid for me."

Though that path seemed winding, she wanted to trust in it, just as she was taught, no matter how difficult that task was.

"Goddess, grant me strength to face my trials."

Aurelia had always been the strong one, the brave one. Nessa was made for comforting, for reassuring, for healing and mending when the adventuring was done. For tending to scraped knees and bruised hearts.

Perhaps it was time she took the leap and scraped her own knees in the process.

"Goddess, fill me with faith that I may live in service to You."

Her entire life in the temple came down to that. A priestess's purpose was clear. She was to follow the Goddess's tenets, strive to do good in the world, and be a living example of Her goodness.

She was no longer a priestess, couldn't be. Did it follow that her life could no longer be in service? That she could no longer be *of* service? If not, then how did a pirate's life fit in?

Nessa took a deep breath and repeated the prayer again then again. She would repeat it until she found clarity. Or perhaps just until something, anything, made sense.

The uneasiness burying itself in her chest reminded her of those times as a child when she and Aurelia wriggled their way through prayer sessions while the older priestesses eyed them with disappointment. At least she'd always been better at silent contemplation than Aurelia, if only by a small margin.

Her heart ached for her old friend.

If Aurelia were here right now, she would say . . . that it didn't matter if she had all the pieces right now. It didn't matter if she knew every bend in the road, only that she was confident in the next step she was taking.

She'd say that perhaps the certainty didn't matter after all.

All her life, Nessa had been like a leaf drifting downstream, at the mercy of the water's flow. The journey was agreeable enough, and it allowed her to appreciate the sights, but as long as she followed the river, she'd never be in control.

Didn't she deserve to have a say in her life? Wasn't that what everyone deserved?

She inhaled deeply and suddenly, as though the realization had hit straight in her lungs. She didn't want to be a leaf in the stream. She wanted to make her own choices. She wanted to make *this* choice. Because she, like everyone, deserved to be in charge of her own life.

Nessa sat at Idir's dining table with Idir and Mallak. Like the rest of the house, it was modest but finely made. If she remained a merchant's apprentice, she could one day rise to his level and have a life this stable and worthwhile, too. As delicious as the dinner had been, dessert was even better, a rich cake with chunks of fruit that started out tart then became sweet.

"Now that the food is mostly gone, we can get to the matter at hand," Idir said once he'd inhaled his slice. "Are you leaving us, Nessa?"

Nessa deflated. "I'm sorry."

"Why do you need to be sorry?" Idir shrugged. "Employees come and go, and though I'll be sad to say goodbye, I know you're doing what is best in your heart."

"How did you know?"

"You've been looking at your aunt's letter every time there's a lull in the shop. Anyone with half a brain could have figured out you've been weighing your options." He waved a hand. "Besides, I'd be more surprised if someone your age *wanted* to stay in the same place forever."

"I really am sorry. I just came to the decision last night."

"You have nothing to apologize for."

"We only wanted to make sure you knew how much Idir has appreciated your presence," Mallak said, "and that you always have a place here if you want it."

Tears stung Nessa's eyes. To have gone from knowing no one on this island to having two friends she could count on was overwhelming. Quietly, she said, "Thank you both."

Idir and Mallak exchanged a touched look, which only overwhelmed her more. Then Mallak nudged Idir, who startled as though he just remembered something, got up, and disappeared into a back room. When he returned a moment later, he carried a rectangular package wrapped in plain cloth.

Sitting down again, he slid it across the table to her. "Here you are, my dear. A going-away present, if you will."

Nessa sucked in a deep breath to ward off the crying. If they kept this up, she might never leave the island.

"Well?" Idir pressed. "Open it!"

She pulled at the twine that tied the wrapping, which fell away to reveal a book of Tiernan's poetry bound in leather with gold leaf. She put a hand to her mouth. It was one of the volumes she'd kept in her room at the temple. Whenever Aurelia got in a temper or an older sister was too hard on her, Nessa would lie next to her and read to her until she calmed down. Often, she read these poems.

"Idir . . ." Her voice cracked on his name. "How?"

"I've seen you reading the shop's copies on your lunch breaks every once in a while," Idir said.

"He's very observant, if you haven't realized that yet," Mallak teased. Seeming to sense she needed a change in the conversation, he said, "Idir told me you recently got a new dagger. May I see it?"

"Of course." Sniffling, Nessa drew it from her belt and held it out for him.

Mallak's smile grew as he studied it. While Idir ran the business, Mallak's specialty was the finer, rarer goods. He twirled it, letting the candlelight twinkle off the blade.

He looked up. "Do you know what kind of weapon this is?"

"I think Occu said it was from Zheyr."

"Yes, that's right. But it's not just any dagger. It's called a beacon blade."

"Ooh-hoo," Idir said with a hearty chuckle.

Nessa looked between them. "Wait. What is that?"

"People would have them commissioned before going on an adventure or a quest," Mallak said. "It was meant to be a reminder of the life and home they were leaving behind and a symbol of the strength they carried with them. It was said to always point them where they needed to be, even if that was back home, although there's not much information on how it would do so."

Idir shrugged. "It's a pretty blade, though. Sharp, too."

"Do you know what the etching says?" she asked.

It was a long shot, but if anyone knew, it would be Mallak. Or he might know whom to ask.

Mallak held the dagger closer to the nearest candle and examined it with narrowed eyes. Nessa had to remind herself to breathe. It had belonged to someone else before, and the words had been meant for that person, not her. They had no bearing on her life.

A moment later, he said, "In love was this blade forged. With love is it wielded. For love will it guide you home."

Nessa felt like someone had stuck her in a vise and squeezed. She couldn't breathe. When Idir walked around the table and wrapped her in a warm embrace, she clung to him.

"When you feel lost," he murmured into her hair, "remember to let love guide you home."

PART 3

Near midday on the fourth day of Kalcetryn, Nessa finally got the courage to walk down to the port, Min at her side. She still wasn't sure why Min wanted to throw in her lot with pirates instead of finding a position as a navigator on a more reputable ship, but if she was going to respect her own right to make choices about her life, she was going to respect Min's, too.

Without a cloud in the sky, the sun seemed extra bright, the scent of salt extra strong today. A stiff breeze blew in from the sea, tousling the strands of hair that were loose from her braid.

"You nervous?" Min asked, her tone light.

Nessa gave a nod, exhaling shakily.

"Remember that she asked you to come. She wants you there."

And once Sabeen got to know her, what then? Would Sabeen want her to *stay* around?

Down at the docks, the churning in her gut grew with each anchored ship they passed. *The Winged Lady*—easily recognizable by its figurehead of a beautiful woman with wings and its flag, which featured a like silhouette—stood tall and proud at the end. Nessa pointed it out as they came closer.

Min let out a low whistle. "Impressive."

"Is it?" Nessa didn't know anything about seacraft.

"Oh, yeah. She's fast. Very fast."

So, her pirate aunt had a nice ship. That was good to know.

When they reached *The Winged Lady*, Min took one look at Nessa's face and led the way up the gangplank. The deck was deserted, which seemed odd. Then again, Nessa didn't know the first thing about being a sailor. She had a lot to learn.

"I wasn't sure you'd come."

Nessa turned. Sabeen descended the steps from the helm. Her coat was forgotten today. Her shirtsleeves were rolled up, the laces undone against the heat of the day. She walked slowly over to them.

"I wasn't sure I would, either," Nessa admitted.

"I'm glad you did." Sabeen turned to Min. "And your friend?"

They shook hands as Nessa introduced them.

"It's good that my niece has found someone who cares enough about her to brave a pirate ship," Sabeen said with a teasing smile.

"I couldn't resist the chance to see her up close," Min said, gesturing to the ship.

Sabeen tilted her head. "A sailor?"

"Navigator for hire."

Sabeen flicked an approving gaze in Nessa's direction. Nessa licked her lips. It was odd—to not need someone's approval and to crave it all the same.

"Where's your crew?" Nessa asked, mostly to shake off that embarrassment.

"Shore leave until tomorrow. We have some time to talk." Sabeen cleared her throat and straightened up. "May I escort you to my quarters? I'll prepare tea."

The room she led them to was more spacious than Nessa expected, even for a captain. A massive mahogany desk was situated in front of a wide window. A burgundy velvet sofa and chairs upholstered in bright patterns reminiscent of waves clustered around an oval table. Bookshelves lined two walls. Each shelf had a lip at the edge to prevent the books from tumbling off due to the motion of the ship. A pair of wooden doors were centered on the right wall, presumably leading to a bedroom.

Sabeen ushered them to the sofa before leaving to fetch the tea. Min settled down, looking at ease with one ankle crossed over her knee and an arm slung around the back of the sofa. Nessa perched nearby, her shoulders tense and her neck tight.

Min smiled. "Remember—the hard part is over."

Nessa blew out a slow breath, relaxing slightly. She had made her decision and, if Sabeen agreed, this would be her new life. There was nothing to be scared of—not the ocean or the crew of *The Winged Lady* or her aunt.

Sabeen returned with a tray that held a pot of boiling tea, three teacups and saucers, and a small assortment of cookies and finger cakes. She placed it on the table before sitting in a chair and pouring out the first cup. She, too, was comfortable and confident, but she was always like that. Was she not burning with anticipation like Nessa was?

Nessa couldn't take it any longer and blurted, "I want to sail with you."

One of Sabeen's eyebrows rose, but her tea-pouring never wavered. "I expected there'd be more small talk, but that's exactly what I'd hoped you'd say."

Nessa's heart lightened. "Really?"

"I wouldn't have offered if I hadn't meant it. You're my brother's child, and we've lost out on so much time already." Sabeen handed Nessa and Min their cups and settled back in her chair, studying them.

Warmth spread to Nessa's cheeks. Blood didn't mean obligation. Blood didn't mean Sabeen owed her anything. To have someone *choose* her—that was everything.

And she wasn't the only one.

"Min, too," Nessa said, "if that's all right."

"Of course." To Min, Sabeen said, "We have a navigator already, but we'll be sure to find a use for you. For both of you."

"Thank you," Min said.

"It will be hard, you understand. A life on the sea is not an easy one. But I promise it will be worth it."

Min nodded. "We're ready."

Nessa, less assured and likely more afraid than Min, would nevertheless face this trial with as much grace as the previous ones. Grace and determination. Determination could take one far.

"Good," Sabeen said. "I'd be remiss if I didn't let you know that I'm not the only one who makes decisions on this ship."

"I thought you were the captain," Nessa said, a furrow in her brow.

"The captain, yes, not a dictator. The majority of the crew has to agree."

Nessa's frown deepened. "Do you think they will?"

"I'm confident, yes," Sabeen answered.

"See? All settled." Min dipped a cookie into her tea. "This is delicious, by the way. Thank you."

Sabeen inclined her head.

Oh, right, she had tea. Nessa blew on hers before sipping it. It tasted of nuts and citrus. She didn't know what food was like on a ship, but at least they had good tea.

Sabeen leaned forward to catch Nessa's eye. "Not entirely settled, I'm afraid."

Nessa set down her teacup and exchanged a quick, reassuring glance with Min.

"To join the crew, officially, you need to complete a challenge. We call it the Trial of the Seafarer."

"What do we have to do?"

"Well, that's sort of up to you. It can be anything that will prove your worth to the crew. Some people have swum the Foskah Channel, some have done brave deeds, some have crafted artwork or mended parts of the ship, some have . . . acquired rare items, so to speak. Oh, Tolush made us a feast with the rarest bird from Ulwendu when he joined. He's the cook now."

"That's . . . a lot."

"The test is meant for you to show off your skills, prove your heart," Sabeen said.

Nessa didn't *have* skills. She had led a sheltered life until everything she'd known was ripped out from under her. She hadn't yet had room to grow into herself. What could she possibly have to offer?

"Being on the sea is about unity, yes," Sabeen continued, animated now. "We'll never survive unless we're acting as a whole. But individually, being a mariner is about choice, possibility. Exploration and discovery. Where will you choose to go with the gifts you have?"

Gifts. She did have one of those. The proof was in the tattoo on her chest, directly over her heart. She held the elemental gift of water.

But how could she use it? And how without giving herself away as a former member of the Order? Those bounty hunters—or others like them—were still out there. She hadn't escaped them only to be caught down the line.

"I'm a good navigator," Min said.

Sabeen grinned. "Good. How will you use that? Don't show us you can go just anywhere. Your destination should be special. It should be . . . immanent."

"Like . . . fated?"

"Exactly."

Sabeen and Min turned to Nessa expectantly.

She was good in the water, even better now that she was mer-blessed and could hold her breath longer than was natural. With that skill, she could dive for oysters and hopefully one would hold a pearl. Pretty, but not all that rare or spectacular.

No. Not a pearl . . .

She looked up at Sabeen. "Can we complete the trial together?"

"An opportunity to exhibit your teamwork." Head cocked, Sabeen considered. "Yes. Yes, I love it."

"What do you have in mind?" asked Min.

"If you can navigate," Nessa said, "I think I can find the wreck of Cadmon the Explorer's ship. Bring back a piece of treasure, something that belonged to him. His compass, if I can find it."

"That was over a hundred years ago, and no one knows where Cadmon's ship went down," Sabeen said, but her expression was curious and open.

"No one above the surface." A smile tugged at Nessa's lips. She couldn't help it. It was an idea to be proud of, even more so if they pulled it off.

Sabeen's grin grew, too. "If you succeed in this, I think the crew would be mighty pleased to see something like that."

Sabeen hadn't been exaggerating—her crew had a vote in whether they had a chance to join. She stood tall on the ship's quarterdeck, hands on the railing as she peered down at her sailors, Nessa and Min on one side of her and Ekvar, his hands crossed over his chest, on the other and two steps behind.

When Sabeen explained their bid to join the band of buccaneers and what they would attempt in that pursuit, more than a few eyebrows raised at the prospect of finding the wreck of Cadmon's ship. Nessa gripped the railing, and her shoulders raised and fell as she took a deep breath and looked out at the men and women below. Despite not knowing them at all, the desire to prove herself to them was a fire in her chest. And when the Goddess granted you fire, Sister Marie used to say, you could choose to feed it or quench it, and quenching it was an arrogant rejection.

Now a shortish man with bushy white eyebrows and a bushier beard that hung below his round belly walked around the loose circle of pirates and handed each two small stones, one blue and one white. Once all the stones were given out, the crewmen passed around an opaque bowl. As each person held the bowl, they dropped one of the two stones into it. White for no, and blue—like the sea—for yes. It was strange, making this choice and then having to give it up into someone else's hands. Many sets of hands.

As if sensing Nessa's emotions, Min took her hand, threaded their fingers together, and gave a light squeeze. On her other side, Sabeen put a hand on her shoulder. Sandwiched between these two women—these women who cared about her, despite all her flaws—Nessa closed her eyes. With them at her side, supporting, she could do this. She *would* do this. They both would.

A few minutes later, the votes were in. The bushy-haired man, whose name was Ganneth, took possession of the bowl, sat down at a small table, and counted out the stones, white to his left and blue to his right. Even from up here, Nessa could see the results.

They were all blue.

They waited for the official count, though, and then Ganneth nodded his head at the captain and gave a thumbs-up gesture.

Grinning, Sabeen sidled between Nessa and Min, grabbed their arms, and held them up in victory.

"It has been agreed that these mariners will test their mettle and, should they prove successful, join our crew!" she shouted. "The Trial shall begin at dawn!"

Nessa was blindfolded. If it hadn't been at her aunt's hands, if Min hadn't been by her side—though Min was blindfolded now, too—she wouldn't have let it happen.

They had sailed through the night, their destination secret. Nessa and Min were given an interior bunk, with no portholes to look out of, and instructions not to leave until they were summoned in the morning. They'd talked until they were exhausted, and now they stood here with mere hours of sleep under their belt and cloth tied around their heads.

"Hands on my shoulders," Sabeen said.

"Why are the blindfolds necessary, again?" Nessa asked.

"Because part of your challenge," Sabeen explained patiently, "is to navigate your way to the wreck of Cadmon's ship without knowing your starting location."

If Nessa could have shot Min an annoyed look, she would have.

Min must have sensed it anyway. "Sorry," she said sheepishly.

"Nothing to be sorry about," Sabeen said. Then she laughed. "Besides, the blindfolds are fun."

She led them up to the deck, walking slowly so they wouldn't trip. Then a handful of crew members helped them into a rowboat, another thing Nessa wouldn't have allowed except at the request of her aunt. Sabeen climbed in with them, and within a few moments, they were paddling away from *The Winged Lady*.

Nessa bit her lip and tried to calm herself by breathing through her nose. What was to come would help determine her future. All she could do was her best. Goddess willed it would be enough.

"Now," Sabeen said after a minute, "rules for the Trial."

"Pirates have rules?" Min asked.

"They're flexible. Anyway, you may use only the supplies we give you, what you carry, and the skills and wits you possess. There's no time limit, although in the event you take more than a week, you'll need to find an inn or somewhere to stay until we're free to come pick you up. Any questions?"

"No," Nessa and Min said in unison.

"Good. There's nothing to fear. We've all done this."

Shortly, their rowboat scraped against sand. Sabeen hopped out, splashing into the water, and dragged the vessel onto the shore.

"Up you get," she said before helping them to their feet and onto solid ground.

Nessa let out a sigh of relief. "Can I take this off now?" she asked, ashamed of the slight whine to her voice. She wasn't accustomed to being in a strange place without her sight, without a way to gauge threats. All she knew was the sand shifting beneath her boots.

"Patience. Not until I've gone," Sabeen said, not without fondness. "Now, hold out your hand."

Nessa did so.

"A candle. We'll be nearby, but we can't always have eyes on you. When you've completed your trial, light it and I'll come."

"How will you know where we are?" she asked.

"I'll know. Min, your hand."

Rustling and movement, and then Min asked, "A bag?"

"It contains what you'll need. Anything else you want to ask before I go?"

Nessa swallowed hard. She should have questions, she should be using this last chance to her advantage, but her mind was completely blank.

Sabeen took hold of her biceps, her touch gentle, and squeezed. "Breathe, Nessa," she murmured.

Right. Stay in the moment. That was what she'd have to do to pull her weight during this challenge. Min's future was on the line, too.

"Well, if there's nothing..." Sabeen pressed a soft, lingering kiss to Nessa's forehead. "I'll be off. Wait ten minutes until I'm gone. The Goddess be with you."

Nessa let out her breath slowly as Sabeen's footsteps retreated and the boat scraped against the shore. She began counting seconds in her head.

"How long do you think it's been?" Min asked.

"Um, about a minute and a half."

"Reckon it's been long enough."

"She said ten minutes."

"She's behind us. So we just won't turn around."

Before she could protest, Min was untying her blindfold.

"See? Nothing to worry about."

"Yeah, all right." But Nessa made sure to keep her back to the shore.

"Let's see what we've got." Min knelt in the sand and opened the leather satchel Sabeen had given her.

A waterskin, enough rations to last them about a week, some smallish square pieces of cloth, two hammocks, a sextant and other unrecognizable instruments, and a map.

"It's not much, but it's a start."

Nessa looked around. The dunes prevented her from seeing much beyond sand and clear blue sky. "Where do you think we are?"

Min followed her lead. "No idea, but we need to figure it out. Then I can use the map to navigate to the shipwreck."

"We still need a boat, though. Do you think there are people on this island? Settlements?"

"Let's go find out."

The early morning sun was already hot enough to scorch. Nessa wrapped a cloth around her forehead as a small measure of protection. Up on the ridge, the sand stretched out before transitioning into grass and a sparse forest. The opposite bank was visible through the trees. The island was tiny.

Even so, they walked the perimeter, not wanting to miss anything of significance. No people, no camps, and certainly no boats.

"You don't happen to recognize this place, do you?" Nessa asked.

"Not familiar in the least." Min shot her a smile. "But I can figure out where we are. Approximately."

"That's great!" She had to remember that this was the part of the challenge that called on Min's talents, not hers. She only had to be patient.

"Except I have to wait until nighttime so I can see the stars."

Oh. Well, they were never going to complete this in a day anyway.

"It doesn't matter how long it takes, right?" Nessa said. "I'm glad you're here to take point on this because I wouldn't have the first clue where to go from here if you weren't."

"I'll be relying on you soon enough. That's why we make a good team."

"It is." Nessa clapped her hands. It was too hot out here to allow a comment like that to send even more heat to her cheeks. "We have at least eight hours until dusk. That gives us ample time to find food and shelter. Which do you want?"

"You hunted and foraged at the temple, didn't you?"

"Yeah, although I'm not sure what, if anything, is hiding on this island."

"You'll still know more than me." Min gestured to Nessa's dagger. "And you've got the blade. You take food, and I'll look for shelter. Meet back here in, say, two hours?"

"Two hours, yeah. Good luck."

Nessa held out her arm, and Min grasped it. It was silly, since they'd reunite so soon, but as she walked away from the beach and into the forest, she couldn't help but smile. They were going to blow Sabeen's expectations out of the water because Min was right—they made a great team.

Temples were self-sufficient, and since the one Nessa had grown up in had a score of sisters at its peak, she knew a thing or two about keeping herself alive through foraging for edible plants and small-game hunting. She knew enough to secure a nice meaty snake within the hour, which would provide dinner as well as leftovers for the morning.

Min had delivered on her assignment, as well, and they now sat beneath a rocky outcrop on the eastern end of the island, the skinned snake roasting over a healthy campfire. Nessa sat with her arms around her tucked-up knees, alternating between keeping an eye on their dinner and looking at the stars.

Min watched the stars, too. Studied them, more like. She had the map and her instruments out as she compared points and made calculations that Nessa, who watched in awe, couldn't hope to comprehend. Min would explain it all if she asked, but Nessa didn't want to break her concentration.

Much later, once Nessa had finished eating and cleaning up and was simply lying in the warm sand contemplating the stars, Min jabbed her finger against the map in triumph.

"I figured it out!"

Nessa sat up. "You know where we are?"

"I do!"

That was incredible—and in only a few hours. On her own, Nessa would have been stranded for days, if not longer.

Min scrambled over, held the map up to the firelight, and pointed to the ocean. "We're here."

"But . . . there's nothing there."

"Not on the map, but I assure you, this is where we are."

"She dropped us off on an actual uncharted island?" Nessa's mouth hung open, but if Min said she was sure, she was sure.

"Your aunt seems invested in making this challenge interesting." She moved her finger east. "The good news is we're quite close to this island, which *is* charted."

"Thank the Goddess," Nessa said under her breath. "How close is it? Can we get there?"

"It is, technically, swimmable."

"I don't like the sound of that . . ."

"It's . . . a little over four miles."

Four miles! And swimming in the open ocean was nothing like swimming in the lakes and rivers back home, especially not that they were getting so close to the part of the Sea of Velk that mariners insisted was inhabited by monsters.

"It'll be all right," Min assured her. "I'm a strong swimmer, and I can help you when you need a rest."

Nessa took a deep breath. She had to remember she was mer-blessed, whatever that truly meant, if anything, beyond her increased lung capacity. "I can do it," she said. "I can."

"Wouldn't doubt it," Min said with a smile. "Then it's settled. We make the journey in the morning."

Nessa gave a nod of agreement. A good night's rest and enough food to break their fast would have to be enough preparation.

Min set the map and tools aside in favor of her portion of the snake. Nessa ran a hand over the smooth paper of the map. It didn't look old, but the creases were well-worn. Did it belong to Sabeen?

"How'd you learn all that anyway?" she asked. "I mean, did you always want to be a navigator?"

Min ate some snake meat, licked the grease off her fingers. "I never really thought about it. My grandparents were fishermen. They taught me. And when I got old enough, after they'd died, I wanted something bigger. Wanted to see the world. So I got an apprenticeship on a cargo ship, left Shanlin, and never looked back."

So, their histories weren't that different. They'd both been left with no one, in a way.

"What were they like?" Nessa asked softly. She didn't want to pry, but she did want Min to know she could be trusted.

"Oh, you know," Min said, "exasperating, doting, intelligent, hardworking. All the usual things. Gave me a good life. And they loved me. That's for sure."

"Sounds nice."

"It was."

"Do you think if they hadn't . . ."

"If they hadn't died, would I have left?" Min finished. "I don't know. I don't know if there's a point to asking things like that, do you? If circumstances were different. But they aren't, and we can't change the past, so worrying about it is pointless."

As Nessa considered that, her next question lodged in her throat. Because she wanted to ask if she had stayed on Tarroga, would Min have stayed with her?

Perhaps Min was right, though. Why rehash the past when there was the present to worry about? There was only right now, and right now, they had a Trial to complete.

The sea roiled.

Nessa stood on the shore, boots sinking into the soft sand. She'd rather do this barefoot, to feel the grains between her toes and the soft lap of the water. Rather do it with fewer clothes on, too, but they had to carry what they were able to. She'd slung a hammock around her chest, half of their possessions tucked inside. Everything would be soaked by the time they reached their destination. Nothing to be done about that, though.

A few miles of ocean were nothing. She could do this, and the Goddess would be with her every stroke of the way. Because if she couldn't believe in herself, how could she expect the Goddess to?

"Are you ready?" Min asked, walking up beside her.

"As ready as I'll ever be."

"Then I'll see you on the other side." Min waded confidently into the water.

Nessa watched until Min had reached the point where the land dropped off and she needed to start swimming in earnest before she followed. With each step, the water seeped farther into her boots, her pack, her clothes. As Dima had said, the water wasn't there to impede her; it didn't wish her ill. Nessa simply had to respect it and welcome it as a friend. Only as a friend would it assist her.

"Goddess, be with us," she prayed softly.

Then she dived.

As always, the ocean welcomed her with open arms, its cool touch revitalizing her weary, searching soul. She was coming alive like a flower opening to the sun. Even so, she had a long swim ahead of her.

As children, Nessa and Aurelia had had a trick for getting through the boring or grueling chores the older priestesses set for them. They would imagine themselves on faraway adventures like in the storybooks.

That wouldn't exactly work here, so instead, she made her mind go blank. She stretched out one arm, pulled her body forward, stretched out the other. Repeat, repeat, repeat. For a time, she closed her eyes and let the current carry her.

Before she knew it, she'd caught up with Min, who had to look twice.

"You're . . . really fast," Min sputtered between breaths, treading water.

If Nessa could have shrugged, she would have. "I like the water."

It felt like where she belonged. Every time she came back to it, it reminded her of that simple fact.

"Well, don't let me hold you back!" Min shouted.

"I'll see you on the other side."

And Nessa returned to her routine—one arm cutting through the water and then the next. All that existed in the entire world was her body and this body of water cradling it. To be one with the sea, she had to give herself to it. It was her; it was the water; and then it was two turned into one.

I give myself to you, and you give yourself to me.

The mantra resounded in her head like a bell with each stroke. The ocean blended into the Goddess so Nessa couldn't tell where one ended the other began. Her heart caught in her chest because for the first real time since leaving the temple, she felt *Her*.

Nessa wasn't alone. Perhaps she never had been.

The sun was high in the sky by the time Nessa made it to the other island. When her feet finally touched sand again, she gave herself a moment to pause and breathe. She swept the hair out of her eyes and wiped the water from her face.

Each step toward dry land was surer, and each one lowered the water level. She was soaked through to the bone. Good thing the day was hot. A few hours out in the sun should dry her pretty thoroughly.

Before that, she walked far enough from shore to survey the island. Some long piers stuck out from the northwestern side, and directly in front of her, about a hundred yards away, was a smallish village. Yes, they'd be able to procure a boat here.

Turning back to the ocean, she unwrapped her pack and laid it and the spare contents out on the ground to dry. Then she sat down in the sand, warm against her skin. She squinted, but Min wasn't visible yet. She would make it here soon.

Her breathing had calmed, but that telltale ache that followed extreme exertion was building in her muscles. She freed her braid from its leather tie, shook it loose so it would dry faster, and lay back. The sand clung to her legs, her arms, her palms. For once, she didn't mind. Each grain was a tiny reminder of her connection to the world.

She closed her eyes against the bright sun. Without meaning to, she dozed, only waking when Min collapsed beside her.

Nessa blinked away her drowsiness. "You made it!"

"Well, don't sound so surprised. I thought I was a fast swimmer till I met you," Min said with a grin. "You had the right idea. It's time for a nap."

Chuckling, Nessa shook her head. "You should get dry first."

Min pillowed her head on her arms and closed her eyes. "Looks like you napped *and* dried at the same time. Why can't I?"

"You can." Nessa patted her on the back and lay down again. "I'll just get a little more sun, then."

Min grunted.

Fine, then. Nessa would let her sleep for a bit.

It was afternoon before Min woke. They nibbled on rations and, still drowsy from the swim and the sleep, sauntered into the village. While purchasing a proper meal would be nice, they needed to use what little money they had wisely. Who knew if it would even be enough?

Nessa let Min lead the way. The village had two streets—one that ran east to west and another north to south—that intersected in the middle. Thatched grass roofs covered wooden buildings, most one-story. People went about their days. A lot of fishermen, from what she could tell, who came here to fill their boats but lived on a bigger, more populous island.

"Should be able to get a boat here," Min said quietly.

"Except we don't have much money," Nessa said back.

"We'll think of something."

Even villages this small had watering holes, this one called The Thirsty Thornfish. An inn with rooms available to rent, it was one of the only two-story buildings. Special rates for fishermen coming to the island for business. Natural light streamed in through the open windows that faced the sea. They had no glass in them like the ones back home, just served as portals to the open air. Tables clustered on the floor, although at this time of the day, only a few of the chairs were occupied.

Min led the way to the bar, which was more like a sanded plank of wood on stick-like trestles, where a woman about a decade older than they were stood to serve them. Gray streaked her dark brown hair, and she wore a sleeveless vest that looked cool in the heat.

She regarded them warily. "Afternoon. What can I do you for?"

"Afternoon," Min said. "Information, actually. Where might we find a boat fit for two?"

The innkeeper's gaze swiped them up and down. "You fishers?"

"Uh, no." Min looked to Nessa.

They hadn't discussed how much they would divulge to people. While pirates were neither universally hated nor universally regarded—it much depended on who one asked—it didn't seem bright to divulge their task to a stranger.

"We're looking for a relic, actually," Nessa said.

"In the ocean?" the woman asked, her head cocked.

"That's right."

The woman let out a long, low whistle. Clearly, she thought they had lost their minds sometime long before this moment. She shrugged one shoulder. "Might know a place."

The moment hung.

The woman rolled her eyes and said plainly, "Buy some drinks, and I'll tell you."

Oh, right.

Min's questioning glance meant the decision was Nessa's, but Nessa only shrugged. There wasn't much of a choice, was there?

Min took two precious coins from their meager pouch and set them on the bar top.

The woman scooped them into her palm, took two mugs from a shelf, filled them with an amber-colored ale, and handed them over. She lifted an eyebrow until Nessa and Min each took a cup and drank deeply.

"It's good," Nessa said, wiping her lip with the back of her hand.

"Ooh, delicious," Min added. "Notes of seaweed, I think?"

The woman finally smiled. "A good palate you have there."

"About that boat?"

"Right. Suppose you could try old Ammie." The woman leaned her forearms on the bar. "Lives on the south side of the island. Sometimes rents out boats to newcomers."

"Thank you," Nessa said.

Min chugged the rest of her drink and thunked the mug back onto the bar. Nessa took some generous sips, but unable to finish it fast enough, she returned it not quite empty.

"Thanks again," Min said.

She bumped Nessa's shoulder, and they headed out.

"One more thing, ladies," the woman called as they reached the door.

They both turned.

"Don't let whatever you're looking for blind you. The sea is more important than any trinket, and she must be respected."

Nessa, suddenly shaky, gave a sharp nod before escaping into the daylight. She paused near the street and looked at Min.

"A bit creepy. I agree," Min said, reading Nessa's face.

Nessa licked her dry lips. "You don't think . . ." She sighed, feeling as though if she voiced her fears aloud, they were more likely to come true.

"I think," Min said, her words deliberate, "if you keep believing in your goddess, she'll be on our side and there's no way we can fail to respect the sea." She held out her hand.

Nessa let the words sink into her. When it came down to it, the Goddess didn't seem all that different from the Grandmother Sea that the mer people spoke of. All she could do was petition the sea and hope the sea granted it.

She took Min's outstretched hand, and they made their way down the south road. Near the shore stood a batch of businesses who promised fresh fish or boats or captains for hire. Ammie's, it turned out, was at the east end of the strip of buildings, set slightly apart. It had seen better days, with some planks off-kilter or missing entirely, and the paint over the door was half-peeled.

Nessa ducked into the open doorway first, Min right behind her. The cramped inside featured no windows, so the only sun came through cracks in the ceiling. In the dimness, some messy shelves, a rocking chair and blanket, and a table with a tea set were visible, but no proprietress.

"Hello?" Nessa said.

"Out here!" someone called from outside.

They followed the voice through a back door that opened onto the shore. A woman sat on a stool, head bent as she sanded an oar. She had seen seventy summers, possibly, her hair a wild shock of white. Her skin was rough and weathered from sun and wind and sea.

"Ammie?" Min asked.

The woman looked up. "That's right! Pleased to meet you."

"Likewise."

Ammie got to her feet with a groan, but she smiled at them. "Body's getting old. It can slow me down, but it can't stop me."

Nessa smiled back. She liked Ammie.

"Now," Ammie said, hands on her hips, "what are you after today?"

Min stepped forward and introduced herself. "We need a boat for a few days, perhaps a week. We were told you might be able to help us."

"Aye, I might. I've got a number of vessels for rent. It's just you two?"

"That's right."

"I've got the just the skiff, I think. She's old, but she'll sail real well for you. Handles like a dream."

"That sounds perfect," Nessa said.

"How far are you going?"

"The eastern Sea of Velk."

"To Mydrost?"

Nessa shook her head. "What we seek isn't on land."

Ammie's face dimmed. "There are monsters in those waters. Don't you know that?"

"We've heard, yes, but we'll be careful."

"Hmm." Ammie ambled over to them. "Let me look at you, children."

She put her hands on Min's face first, locking gazes and studying her for a long moment. Min endured the unusual scrutiny without blinking.

Ammie let out another small *hmph* sound before moving to Nessa and repeating the process. The old woman's hands were rough on her cheeks, but Nessa didn't mind. Her eyes were a clear cerulean, as though she could view the depths of the ocean in them.

Finally, Ammie dropped her hands and drew away. "I see," she murmured to herself. To Nessa and Min, she said, "I don't need to know what it is you seek. What I know is you're brave young ladies and your intentions are pure. That's enough for me. You may rent my vessel. There is, however, one thing to know before you do. Respect the sea, and she will take care of you."

That sounded much less threatening than how the innkeeper had worded things.

Nessa stepped forward. "Thank you, Ammie. We promise."

"Aye."

Min took out their purse and dumped their coins into her palm, a meager showing. "I'm afraid this is all we have."

"It's hardly enough for a night at the inn," Ammie said, scratching her chin. "Tell you what. Lubin has a supplies shipment for me, but he's at the north end of the island. The bastard insists he doesn't have enough employees to bring them 'round to this side. Fetch them for me, and the boat's yours for the next few days."

A day's work for transportation seemed more than an even exchange.

"Mind you," Ammie added, "some of it's heavy, and he's not going to help you load any of it."

A hard day's work, then. Once again, Min left the decision up to her.

"That works for us. We'll do it," Nessa said and shook Ammie's hand.

An hour later, sweat dripped down Nessa and Min as they loaded a humongous coil of sailing rope into Ammie's cart beneath the boiling sun. Even with a cloth wrapped around her head, it trickled down Nessa's forehead and stung her eyes. Between loads, Nessa ripped the sleeves off her tunic in an effort to cool down. She replaced the damp cloth on her head with one of the sleeves.

"Sutkey," she cursed, leaning on the cart. Her chest heaved as she tried to catch her breath.

"Yeah, shit," Min agreed. She bent over, hands on her knees. Through labored breaths, she asked, "You think this is worth it?"

Nessa focused on her breathing. It was only day two of their Trial of the Seafarer. Who knew how many days lay ahead? And each seemed likely to be more difficult than the last.

Still, the difficult made it more worth it. Didn't it?

"I think there's only one way to find out," she said. "You don't want to quit now, do you?"

"Not a chance," Min said with a grin. "We do this together."

"Yeah."

Nessa wiped her face with her torn-off sleeve to hide her expression. She hadn't had a "together" with someone since Aurelia had left the temple for the capital. For a long time, she thought she never would, and shortly, they might be accepted by an even larger group. Perhaps, it could even be like having a family.

Min slapped her bicep. "Come on. A few more hours' work, and we'll be done."

Nessa didn't need to be told twice.

When they'd delivered the supplies to her establishment, Ammie fed them a simple supper of fish, fruit, and grain. The filling meal helped ease Nessa's aching muscles. Afterward, she led them to her modest boatyard. The sun had almost met the horizon, casting the world in a pinkish gold haze and sending sparks of light over the rippling water.

Over half the berths were empty, their vessels rented out. Ammie took them to a short jetty off to the side, where only one boat was moored. It was a beautiful craft. Nessa didn't know much about boats, but she knew that much. Carved from smooth, dark wood, it featured a magnificent, majestic whale in silver etching. She didn't look old at all, but well cared for.

"Here she is," Ammie said, "as promised."

"What's her name?" Nessa asked.

"*Velmurai*. It means *Blessing of the Water*."

Relief swept through Nessa. After all the talk today of respecting the ocean, this seemed like a good portent. She ran a hand over the boat's hull. A gorgeous piece of craftsmanship.

"Thank you, Ammie. Truly," Min said.

"Aye. You can thank me by coming back safe, you hear?"

It was rare—and beautiful—to find care and connection in a stranger. Perhaps that was part of the Trial, to illustrate the beauty in the world that Nessa so often closed her eyes to unknowingly.

"We will," she promised.

Ammie clapped each of them on the shoulder before directing them to a copse of palm trees near the water where they could set up their hammocks for the night. By the time they hung them in a V shape, with their heads close together, the sun was down and the stars were out.

Only when it was dark could Nessa give voice to the tiny seed of fear inside her chest. In a whisper, she asked, "What if it's not even down there?"

Outside of the gentle crash of the waves, the night was so, so quiet. Or perhaps it just seemed that way because Nessa was holding her breath.

"It will be," Min said, her words soft but resolute.

But what if it's not? Nessa wanted to ask again.

Min reached out in the dark and took hold of Nessa's hand. "Even if it's not, there's always a way, and we'll find it."

And Nessa, believing her, breathed freely once more.

They left with the rising of the sun. For most of the morning, Min showed Nessa the basics of sailing—hoisting the sail, securing it, steering the boat, caring for it. All knowledge she would need, albeit on a bigger scale, on *The Winged Lady*.

At midday, the ocean was smooth, and they were able to sit, eat the lunch Ammie had packed for them, and bask in the sun while the wind blew the ship onward.

"Are you ready for this?" Min asked between bites of orange.

Nessa tried for bravado. "I have to be, don't I?"

"Sure, but . . ." Min's brow wrinkled. "Do you even know how far down it is?"

Nessa closed her eyes against the brilliantly blue sky. She knew more than most about the ocean, but she didn't know this. If the past two years had taught her anything, it was that she rarely, if ever, could guess correctly at the future. That had to be by design. She could plan so far, but the Goddess would take her where She willed. And if the Goddess had brought her this far, surely She would see her through to the end.

No matter how deep the wreck of Cadmon's ship lay.

Nessa had to trust that. Trust *Her*.

"No," she admitted, "but however deep it is, that's how far I'll have to go."

"And your magic will help with that?"

Would it? The gift was dying and had been for longer than she'd been alive. What knowledge that remained was limited to the most basic of magic. Yet she felt the stirrings of *something* within her each time she touched the water.

"I hope so," she finally said.

"If it's too far down," Min said, "you'll stop, right? You'll come back?"

Nessa traced the bob of her throat with her gaze and blushed. She wasn't accustomed to being cared for, looked after. Perhaps she should allow herself to grow used to it, though. Everyone deserved that, even her.

"Is that what you want me to do?" she asked.

Min ran a hand over her hair and leaned back with a sigh. "It's not my decision, and I won't be the one to keep you from completing the Trial—"

"It's your Trial, too."

"I know. But you have the harder part."

Nessa couldn't have made it this far without Min, but this didn't seem the moment to protest.

"In the end, it'll be your call to make," Min said finally, "but promise me that you'll be careful, that you'll remember to watch out for yourself."

Nessa nodded. That was something she could do. "I promise."

They sailed through the day and into the night, finally dropping anchor when Min began to struggle to stay awake. The open ocean was breezier than the islands, so they curled up beside one another in blankets from *Velmurai's* modest storage compartment.

Even with their separate rooms, Nessa had spent many a night sleeping beside Aurelia before she left the temple. Since then, she'd slept alone, just like she did everything. Now, as she lay on the hard planks of a rocking boat, her back against Min's, tears burned her eyes and a lump formed in her throat. Instead of bottling it up as she normally did, she relaxed. She let the tears flow. Because for the first time in far too long, she felt safe. Min, like Aurelia, was someone she could trust implicitly.

She felt safer still in the arms of the water that surrounded them. If she just held onto this feeling, held onto this certainty, they would realize their goal. Their faith would make them unstoppable.

At midmorning the next day, Nessa helped Min strike the sail. They were close to where they needed to be, and full wind could push them too far. She turned the crank to lower the anchor before settling to wait as Min consulted her maps and tools to get their bearing. It was as though she spoke a different language. Perhaps Nessa would learn the art of navigation one day. For now, she was content to watch.

After a long while, Min set aside her instruments and looked Nessa straight in the eye. "We're here."

Nessa wouldn't insult her by asking whether she was sure. The time had come for her part of the Trial. Goddess be with her.

"All right," she said evenly.

She removed her boots and socks, stuffed her socks inside her boots, and tucked them beneath a bench. She wriggled her bare toes against the boat's planking. That left her in her sleeveless tunic, trousers, and belt with her dagger looped into it. She redid her braid to make sure her hair wouldn't obscure her vision.

Suddenly, there was nothing more to be done.

Min seemed to feel it, too. "We can take some time," she said. "You don't have to dive this second."

Nessa reassured her with a smile. "There's no time like now."

The sooner she went down, the sooner she would be back up here.

"All right," Min said, nodding to herself, "all right."

Even with a refreshing breeze, the day was hot and the air was heavy. Nessa could hardly swallow. She swigged from a waterskin and rolled her shoulders to loosen the muscles.

Next came the dive stone strapped to her back. It would pull her down faster than she could swim, meaning more time to search for the wreckage and then for the compass. The ropes slipped around her shoulders so that when the time came to resurface, she could rapidly drop the weight.

Ready, Nessa perched on the port side, back toward the sea, hunched forward so the dive stone wouldn't drag her off the boat too early. Once she dove, there would be no good way to ensure communication between them.

Min was putting on a brave face, but even her recent exposure to the sun couldn't hide how pale it was right now.

"Hey," Nessa said, voice gentle, "you got us this far. I'll get us across the finish line."

"You better," Min said with a teasing grin. "First sign of trouble—"

"And I'm on my way back to the surface. I promise."

"Good."

Gripping the edge of the railing, Nessa closed her eyes and took three long, deep breaths, one for each line of the prayer.

Goddess, guide my steps down the path You've laid for me.

Goddess, grant me strength to face my trials.

Goddess, fill me with faith that I may live in service to You.

Without opening her eyes, she said, "See you on the other side," took a last deep breath, and tipped backward off the boat.

The world went quiet. It might have scared a different person, but not someone with the ocean in her veins.

She flipped herself as the stone pulled her down, and it was mere moments before her feet touched the bottom, sending the sand up in a puff. She waited for it to settle again. Fish were scuttling away from her, but no wreck of a ship in that direction.

She turned in a slow circle, and her heart lit up. There it was, about fifty yards away, but there it was. Min had gotten them *so* close. It was incredible.

She walked forward. The ship was gorgeous, much larger than the one that waited for her on the surface. It lay tipped over. The current and sea life had rotted much of the wood, but the substantial holes that had been torn into its hull were clearly visible. Perhaps the stories of a kraken attack, accidental or not, were true after all. Ammie certainly believed monsters lurked in these waters.

Cadmon's compass. That was what she was after. It would likely be in the captain's quarters. Before she entered the wreck, she sloughed off the dive stone.

The quarters were about what she expected based on Sabeen's—furniture, a desk, cabinets, everything dilapidated from a century beneath the sea. She searched methodically in order not to miss anything. The compass would be small and easy to overlook. But methodical also meant slow and the desk and cabinets held so many compartments. With each one she searched, her heart sank lower. Where was it?

Cadmon's skeleton lay in a chair in the corner. At least, she assumed it was Cadmon. His clothes, mere flaps of red and blue cloth now, waved in the water. All in all, he looked like he'd met a peaceful end. The gold necklace around his bony neck was a coin, not a compass. Nor was the compass on the rest of his person or lying nearby.

Her breath was running out. This dive was done. She swam her way out of the bowels of the ship, back into the open ocean, and up toward the surface. With each stroke, the light came closer. She couldn't be certain, but it felt as though the sea was buoying her upward. Even so, her lungs were nearly empty when she broke through the surface.

She gulped in air.

"Nessa!"

Nessa rotated and groaned. Min and the boat were much farther away than she'd have liked. She began swimming in their direction.

Min was already pulling up the anchor. "No, stay there! I'll come to you."

Nessa stopped swimming. There was a heaviness in her limbs already, and she needed to save her strength, so she floated on her back. Closing her eyes, she let the arms of the sea rock her, allowed her breath to settle into its embrace. No matter how many times the sea asked her to, she would give herself to the water.

Min steered the skiff within five feet of her and dropped anchor again. She scrambled over to the port side and reached for Nessa. Nessa went willingly, letting Min pull her up to she could rest against the side of the boat.

"Do you want to come up?" Min asked.

"No. I need to go back down."

Min grabbed onto her arms for extra security. "What did you see? Is it there?"

Nessa wiped water out of her eyes. "*The Breath of the Naiad*'s there, all right. But visibility's not great, and the inside of the ship is even dimmer."

"You find the captain's quarters?"

Nessa nodded.

"Good. That's a start. Hopefully it'll be out in the open somewhere."

If only. Her breathing had returned to normal. Time to try again.

She tapped a palm against the boat. "Here I go."

Before she could let go of the boat, Min squeezed her forearm. "Be careful."

"I will."

This time, the dive stone took her almost directly on top of the wreck of *The Naiad*. She landed with her feet solidly beneath her, shouldered off the stone, and headed for the captain's quarters.

When she ducked between the staircases toward the cabin, a shadow slithered across the open doorway.

She stopped, stifling a gasp of surprise. It was nothing to worry about. Probably. Most likely, it was the shifting of the light as it came through the water. It definitely wasn't the spirit of Cadmon the Explorer, who had been stuck in this watery grave for a hundred years. She took the dagger out of her belt anyway and held it at the ready.

She spent the next few minutes investigating the cabin to no avail. If *The Naiad* had taken the compass down with it, it was elsewhere on the ship.

She swam down to the lower deck and made her way—through the crew quarters, storage compartments, and finally the galley—as methodically as possible without wasting undue time. Still nothing.

Where could it be? Perhaps it wasn't here at all. Perhaps Cadmon had given it away before his last voyage.

The Breath of the Naiad was here, though, right where Dima had confirmed it would be. That had to mean something.

But right now, she was out of time. She swam through the closest open hatch and toward the surface. She didn't get very far before something brushed against her leg. Her heart lurched, and she startled at the shadow behind and beneath her, the dagger slipping from her grip.

Sutkey.

As she twisted around and squinted, the shadow resolved into the form of an octopus, who stretched out a tentacle and curled it around her leg. Then he uncurled it, gave her a few experimental pokes, and drifted away.

Just a curious little fella, then.

She looked past him, but her blade had disappeared into the depths. No time to go back for it now, not with her lungs burning for air. Turning back to the surface, she kicked her way upward.

Min was ready for her, stretching out to take her by the arms and haul her toward the *Velmurai*. She took one look at her pallid face and said, "I don't think you should go down again."

"One more time," Nessa panted, shaking her head as she hung from the side of the boat. "One more."

She was so close that could she feel it. It had to be down there. She wouldn't give up now.

Min closed her eyes and scrubbed her face with her hands. "All right, but you need to rest first. Give it an hour. And drink some water."

"Half an hour."

Min scoffed. "Fine." She pulled Nessa onboard.

Nessa's limbs were jelly. It was logical that each dive would be harder, but she hadn't factored in how exponentially. The third one, the last one, seemed as likely to kill her as it was to hand her victory.

Min covered her in a towel, rummaged through their packs, and shoved food into Nessa's lap. "Can you sit up?"

"Yeah. Yeah." Nessa let Min help her into a sitting position, wrapped the towel around her shoulders, and dug into an orange. "Stop hovering," she ordered, a teasing lilt to her voice. "You're making me nervous."

Min frowned but nevertheless settled down on a seat. After a moment, she asked, "Where's your dagger?"

Nessa spoke through a mouthful of orange. "Dropped it."

"Is that why you want to go down again?"

"I want to go down again to get the compass."

With luck, she'd find her dagger, too. She presented Min with a section of orange. A peace offering. One more dive, one more try. Right now, she couldn't think about what would come next if she failed. Despite the weight on her shoulders, she was calm. Because she was right where she was meant to be.

Min accepted the slice and popped it into her mouth.

Half an hour went by, and Nessa couldn't wait any longer. Her arms and legs, though not fully recovered, at least no longer shook. Min strapped another dive stone to her back, and she sat on the edge of the boat for one final attempt.

Nessa closed her eyes. "Be with me," she said under her breath, speaking to both the Goddess and the Sea. Perhaps they were one and the same. Perhaps, if they liked her enough, they would lead her where she needed to go.

Before she could second-guess herself, she tipped backward. After even the brief stint in the heat, the coolness of the water refreshed her. That was the final piece of hope she needed. By the time she touched down on the ocean floor, certainty had filled her, and within a heartbeat, a twinkling light beckoned to her from a porthole.

She swam toward it, gripping the sides of the window to peer through. The glint wasn't a random piece of treasure or equipment; it was her dagger. A good portent indeed.

She propelled herself upward and over the main deck and found the nearest hatch. She pulled on the metal loop that opened it. Stuck. She braced her feet against the planks, handle between her legs, and heaved. It lifted.

She dove into the lower deck hallway and into the first chamber she came across. There was her dagger, though how it had ended up here was a mystery. The words etched into the handle glistened like they were on fire.

In love was this blade forged. With love is it wielded. For love will it guide you home.

She reached for the beacon blade, and her hand brushed a small metal chest, about the size of her forearm.

Locked.

She gathered it under one arm and swam back up to the deck. The light, slightly less dim up here, allowed her to inspect the chest more closely. The wooden slats it was made out of were reinforced with iron bands, now rusted. The letters *C* and *M* were etched into the top. She tried the lid, but it was locked.

Her limbs were growing heavier, and there was the slightest of burns developing in her lungs. The chest looked promising, but if it didn't hold the compass, her luck might be running out.

She jammed her blade into the crease of the box and pried. Once, twice, and on the third, the wood splintered and the chest popped open. Inside on a bed of black velvet lay some handfuls of unrecognizable coins, a ring set with a firestone, and a star-shaped pendant. And there, a brass compass, the words *May the Stars Guide You Home* etched on the back.

Nessa slammed the chest shut, tucked it beneath her arm, and darted for the surface. With one arm out of commission and a dagger in her other hand, the going was slow. Plus, now that the end was in sight, the exertion of the past hour was catching up to her. Her limbs felt as heavy as if they were made out of stone, and the pressure in her chest was building. Each stroke heightened her exhaustion until it was so great that she nearly wanted to cry and give up. And the surface seemed impossibly far away.

She couldn't give up now, though, not when she was so close to her goal. With one last expulsion of energy, she kicked herself upward.

At last, at last, she broke through the water and gulped in a big breath of pure air.

Thank you, Goddess, she prayed. *Thank you, Grandmother Sea. Thank you, thank you, thank you.*

Min was right there, reaching to help her into the skiff.

"Take the box, take the box," Nessa urged, panting.

Min did so and, as soon as she saw what it was, said, "Oh, shit."

Nessa's laugh bubbled up through her lack of breath. "Yeah." She was hanging onto the boat, waiting for enough strength to return to pull herself aboard.

As soon as Min quickly but reverently set the chest onto the deck, she leaned over the side, grabbed Nessa around the waist, and heaved her up and into the ship. They collapsed together on the bottom of the boat.

Nessa rolled away and fell on her back. "I think maybe we should take a nap."

Min's laugh was boisterous and delighted. "You've certainly earned it. Get dry first, and then you can sleep as long as you like."

"I don't think I can get up."

"A dry shirt, at least."

Min took her by the underarms and hauled her into a sitting position. She wrapped a towel around her shoulders, squeezed her into a hug from behind, and dropped a quick kiss to her hair. A moment later, she helped Nessa out of her sodden tunic and into the dry one. Then she placed a pillow behind Nessa's head and settled down across from her. Cadmon's chest sat on the deck between them.

Nessa wanted to close her eyes, but she kept her gaze on Min, whose deliriously happy expression undoubtedly mirrored her own as she opened the box and examined the contents.

"You did it," Min said in awe. "You really did it."

"I did," Nessa said. With a lot of determination and just as much help. Her body was heavy and light at the same time, filled with exhaustion and euphoria. This was her first real accomplishment since being abducted. The first one in her whole life, perhaps.

She allowed her grin to blossom. "You did it, too."

"I guess we did it together," Min conceded.

Nessa, breathless still, closed her eyes. "I guess we make a damn fine team."

All told, the journey back to Ammie's dock on the island seemed like a dream. The wind was with them, and they made it by the following evening. Ammie greeted them like old friends, with hugs and supper. Afterward, they lit Sabeen's green candle and went to sleep beneath the stars again, the compass tied around Nessa's neck with a cord.

The Winged Lady appeared on the horizon the following morning. Who knew how close they had been? Sabeen never had explained the candle or how it worked. When the rowboat came to fetch them, only Sabeen and Ekvar were in it. Ekvar stayed near the water once ashore, leaving Sabeen to approach them alone.

She embraced Nessa first, and Nessa sank into it, hungry for her aunt's touch, for her approval. Tears stung her eyes as Sabeen squeezed her tight. She offered Min a hug, too, though hers wasn't quite as lengthy.

"Dare I ask?" Sabeen said playfully when she pulled away.

Nessa gave way to the cockiness that wanted to come out in her smile, reached beneath her tunic, and pulled out Cadmon's compass.

Sabeen shook her head in amazement. "Well done, sailors. Very well done, indeed."

Once again, Nessa found herself standing on the quarterdeck beside Sabeen. Min stood at Sabeen's other shoulder while the crew looked on from the main deck. This time, the sun was setting. This time, the air was ripe with excitement, and Nessa found herself wanting to share in it.

Sabeen took her hand and Min's. "Tonight," she shouted, "we welcome two brave young women, Nessa and Min, who have successfully completed the Trial of the Seafarer. Tonight, we welcome our new crewmembers!"

A more succinct speech than the one a week prior, but an even more welcome one.

The pirates erupted in cheers. Apparently, much like anyone else, they enjoyed any excuse to party. By the time Nessa, Min, and Sabeen walked down the stairs to the main deck, a few had already begun to play lutes, drums, and even something called a hurdy-gurdy. Soon enough, the drinking and dancing commenced.

And it all felt . . . nice. It felt *really* nice. It felt like a safe harbor after being adrift for so long.

As a new crewmember, Nessa and Min's first order was to get a tattoo. Sabeen sat them down in a corner, where a woman named Tree and a man Goby stuck them repeatedly with needles dipped in ink. Nessa grimaced through it, even after Sabeen foisted liquor on them and Min gripped her hand for mutual support.

Despite the pain, she emerged with a smile and a drawing of Cadmon's compass on her forearm. Min's matched.

"A memento of your Trial and your success," Sabeen said, "but also a reminder—sometimes, only when we're lost can we discover who we truly are. This is so you'll always find your way home."

Home. It sounded so simple when she said it. But Nessa hadn't been a part of anything bigger than herself for a long time. Now that she was again, the persistent ache in her chest had receded like the tide.

While the party continued, Sabeen took Nessa's hand and led her below deck to her quarters.

"I'm so proud of you," Sabeen said once they were alone, "and so very happy you've chosen to make your life with us."

"Me, too," Nessa said, meaning it.

"You'll thrive here."

Nessa hoped so. She and Sabeen and Min and the Goddess and perhaps even Grandmother Sea—they would all make sure of it.

She ran a finger over her new tattoo. "What you said, about discovering ourselves when we're lost . . ." She licked her lips, hesitant.

Sabeen nodded patiently, encouraging her to go on.

Nessa didn't quite know how to phrase it, wasn't even sure she could explain it at all. "That's how I feel. When I'm in the ocean. Like I'll never be lost again."

"Like the ocean itself is in your veins?" Sabeen said sagely.

"Yeah." The word came out as a sigh.

Sabeen opened a drawer to her desk and took something small out of it. When she walked closer, Nessa saw it was a silver ring.

Sabeen held it out to her. "This was your father's, his seal as a baron. I think you should have it."

Nessa's smiled dropped in surprise. Sabeen placed the ring in her palm. It was heavy for something so small. Impressed upon the flat top was an image of a fish beneath a crown. Had he loved the ocean as she did?

A question for another night, perhaps. In this new life, there was all the time in the world to ask her aunt about her father. For tonight, she would enjoy the company of friends, both old and new.

She squeezed the ring before sliding it onto her thumb. "Thank you."

"You're welcome," Sabeen said, dipping her head. "Now, let's go enjoy the festivities."

Smiling, Nessa turned to go. She stopped near the door. "Oh, that book I left with you—"

"Safe in your new bunk," Sabeen assured her. "It'll be waiting for you when you go to sleep tonight."

Nessa, a lump in her throat, twisted the ring that had belonged to her late father, thought of the surrogate father who'd given her that book, looked at the very real aunt right across from her. After losing her home and her family, she was so, so lucky to have found those again.

"Thank you," she managed to say again, her voice wavering.

Sabeen, seeming to understand the weight of the words, only smiled.

Back on deck, Tree, Goby, and others pushed drinks into their hands and dragged them into the middle of the deck to dance. The sun had gone down fully by now. Prickles of stars sparkled in the sky, and the moon shone brilliantly, and the whole spectacular firmament was reflected in the inky water. With the buzz in her veins from the tattoo, the buzz in her head from the alcohol, and the buzz in her heart from the atmosphere, it was the most magical experience of Nessa's life.

With one hand resting on the hilt of her beacon blade, she wove her way through the crowd toward Min to share it with her.

ABOUT THE AUTHOR

Carrie Gessner received a BA in English from Carnegie Mellon University and an MFA in Writing Popular Fiction from Seton Hill University. She writes fantasy and science fiction and drinks a lot of tea. She's written three novels and one collection of short fiction.

Her short stories have appeared online at *The Teacup Trail, Freeze Frame Fiction,* and *The Future Fire* as well as in the anthologies *Beautiful Lies, Painful Truths, Death Magic, Dragons of a Different Tail, Fall into Fantasy 2018, Gunsmoke & Dragonfire, Reign, Reign of Queens, The Secrets of Harrowgate Valley,* and *Whispers in the Dark.*

She also cohosts the *Positively Pop Culture* podcast with fellow author K.W. Taylor.

Outside of writing, she enjoys making crafts and building models, playing Dungeons & Dragons or trying new board games and TTRPGs, and outdoor activities like hiking, disc golfing, and taking walks with her greyhound. You can find her online at www.carriegessner.com.

Continue reading
for an excerpt from
The Dying of the Golden Day
(The Heartfriends #1)

Chapter One

Build your life with wisdom, courage, and
compassion, for these are the strongest foundations.

- The Book of the Goddess

The ancient longsword glimmered in the morning
sunlight that streamed in through a colored-
glass window that depicted Lucia, the first
queen of the united land, on her throne. As
though waiting for its true master to reclaim it, for the
day it would rise up to defend the land once more,
Aenlic lay on a stone altar beneath the midnight blue
and silver eagle banner of the Penarvid family. Gold
letters etched into the blade—*I am thy salvation.* On
the underside, unseen—*I am thy downfall.*

Aurelia reached out, fingers trembling, drawn to it.
How many kings and queens had it served? How
many dynasties did it witness rise and fall? How many
secrets did the aged steel hold?

Nothing blocked her path. She could take it now,
deliver it to Renfred, and change the course of history.
Whether he came stealthily or whether he came
marching through the city gates demanding the
throne—if he held this sword, no one would dare
refuse. He was meant to be king, meant to rule this
land and unite it, and she was meant to be by his side
as he did so.

"Sist—" A throat clearing. "Excuse me."

She adjusted the medicine bag on her shoulder, tucked her hand back into the fold of her traveling cloak, and turned to face Turstin, the head physician of the Penarvid family. A short, dour man, his ruddy cheeks reddened even more so under her gaze.

He dipped his head respectfully. "My apologies. But time is short. Perhaps if you would like to examine the sword afterward . . ."

He gestured toward the doorway, and she followed him from the hall and into the corridor.

"I am thankful I located you," he said.

"Why wait until the situation was dire?"

The majority of the temples, including the one in which she was raised, lay abandoned, the acolytes of the Most High Goddess having migrated to those few that hadn't been left to ruin. Turstin had written to all of them.

"You are young, much younger than I imagined," said the physician, "too young, I think, to recall the day this country renounced the Goddess and Her Order. Ill or not, he is still my king, and I would not go against his orders unless as a last resort."

Not an easy thing to forget, even for a child of only three or four summers. Not easy to forget how Sister Morran's anger distorted her normally tranquil expression, how Sister Ruya raged about her workroom until the herbs and plants were strewn all about. Soon after, her temple had gained half a dozen sisters, refugees from Temidorus.

He opened a door flanked by two guards and led her into a dark room that stank of death. The thick velvet curtains were drawn, and the only light came from the hearth and some candles, already burning low and throwing flickering shadows on the walls. They barely illuminated the figure lying in the bed, a man who looked decades older than the fifty-five years she knew him to possess. Turstin and physicians were no longer hoping for his recovery, only waiting for his expiration. Her summons was a last grasp at an impossible hope, the final attempt of a man who knew he was beaten. *She* was his impossible hope, she who'd been plucked from the temple before her skills could truly develop. Still, the ink on her chest bound her to try.

She crossed the room, threw aside the curtains, and opened the window to let in a spray of light and air. "Why do you keep the room like this?"

"There has been some division over how to treat this," said Turstin, facing her from the opposite side of the bed. "Once we realized that our customary methods weren't leading to improvement, some among us began to question the nature of the illness."

"Some think it unnatural?"

"Yes, a dark spirit or some such."

That explained the closed windows, the darkness. "That's unlikely." As the Goddess had abandoned humanity, no longer did the Chortove send his souls to wreak havoc on the earth.

He regarded her with a frown. "Yes, but . . . we are running out of theories."

Aurelia leaned forward to examine the ailing monarch. King Aras slept restlessly, shivering, his frame wasted with sickness. Since the Schism, Aras's Temidorus and her own Sunniva had been on icy terms. She heard tell of him in both the temple and the castle, of his early confidence and grace, of his later descent into madness and mistrust. And she saw him once when she was still only a girl. She and Renfred, barely a year into their heartfriend bond, followed reports of Aras's arrival in a village near the river that divided the two countries. Even from the opposite bank, he'd struck an impressive figure on his black destrier, his broad shoulders taut with restrained power. Everything a king ought to be.

She didn't understand then that every king must fall, that there was always another, a man of honor, a prince in blood and in heart, ready to rise and take his place. Even the greatest of rulers must bend his knee to the law of time.

She pressed the back of her hand to his forehead, unsurprised to feel the clamminess of fever. Gently, she slid his eyes open. The hazel iris was clear. A good sign.

She let his eyelids drift closed again. "Exactly how long has he been like this?"

The wrinkle in Turstin's brow deepened. "Weeks now, perhaps five." He rolled down the blankets and lifted the king's tunic to reveal bandages yellowed with pus. "A hunting accident. It should have healed easily, but infection caught, and none of our usual methods has worked."

Almost if it were no infection at all. Perhaps there was some truth to the physicians' strange theories.

"We've drained the pus and kept the wound clean. Yarrow for his fever, calendula to draw out the infection, samoly to speed the healing." He paused until she looked up. "But we are mere physicians and this has proven to be beyond our abilities."

And he hoped it would not be beyond hers. Dread crept in, fast and weighty. "Healing is not miracle-working, you understand," Aurelia said.

It was nothing but herbs and hope.

"I do," he said, "but if there's anything, anything at all you can . . . Well, this kingdom isn't prepared to lose its monarch."

"No kingdom ever is," she murmured.

Turstin's soft noise was no real reply. When she turned to him, he was staring at the king with sorrowful eyes. "I can trust you, bound to the Goddess as you are. Word of this cannot leave the castle."

"Understood." Understood, but not agreed to. She would take news to Renfred, would betray this man's trust faster than an eagle could snatch its prey. A twinge of guilt pierced her heart.

a heart consumed by darkness

She removed her bag from her shoulder and set it on the floor beside the bed. "I'll need a basin of water and some fresh bandages. And privacy."

He cleared his throat and said, "Of course," before dipping his head and exiting, black physician garments swishing out of sight.

Aurelia waited until the retreat of his boots echoed down the corridor before letting out a sigh and returning her attention to the patient. If a king could become this shrunken, ailing skeleton, then what hope was there for the rest of them? No man should have to die like this, stripped of all his youthful glory, unable to complete his life's work—not for lack of effort but for want of time. He was not her king, but he was not her enemy, either. She didn't wish such an end for him.

Even so, there was a miniscule wicked part of her soul—*the darkness that lives inside you*—that knew if he died today, by her hand, Renfred could step in with no resistance, with barely more than a score of soldiers at his back. With no heir to lead, the citizens wouldn't oppose a benevolent prince whose only wish was to assist a neighboring kingdom through its period of turmoil. Serving her prince was a mark of goodness and duty, not of darkness.

The overlapping circles of ink that formed a flower above her heart warmed. Duty to her Goddess superseded duty to her prince. She must do what she could for Aras, even if it meant Renfred's day would not come as soon as he would prefer.

She took a few slow, deep breaths to calm her pulse. She had overestimated herself, and Renfred had, as well. She didn't want this responsibility, couldn't handle it. A man's fate was not for mortals to decide. It was the Goddess's choice. It was She who bent each man's steps toward his destiny. It was She who should bear the blame.

torn

you are torn

Aurelia crossed to the open window and stuck her head through to inhale a deep lungful of morning air mingled with the pungency of dung. It reminded her that the man dying in the bed behind her was tangible, no figment of her mind. She looked down on the city below, on Temidorans taking their goods to the marketplace. She was the only one left to help their king. She'd grown up believing the Goddess worked through the gifted. Head clear, she returned to her task.

She retrieved a small blade from her bag and gently cut off the old bandages. Yellowed with pus, they looked like they hadn't been changed for days, though with an infection this bad, it was possible they'd been fresh only a few hours ago. She tossed them in a ceramic basin to be burned. Beneath the dressing, necrotic tissue seeped with purulent drainage. The foul stench burned her eyes. The wound ran a hand's length diagonally across the left side of his abdomen. It was not deep enough to cut through the muscle to the organs, but the skin surrounding it bloomed red. Unnatural, indeed.

She swallowed thickly. It'd been a long time since a sister of the Order could deal with anything but the smallest illness.

Her breath hitched as she stretched out her hands, one on top of the other, and held them above Aras's heart. She closed her eyes. As she concentrated, her power welled up within her, starting from a spark and igniting to blossom outward and suffuse her until it radiated from her fingertips.

Her voice was deeper and rougher than normal when the words tumbled from her mouth.

Goddess, grant unto me this man's suffering to save his body and to save his soul.

She waited for a response. For a tense moment, the only sound in the room was the king's raspy breathing and her own heartbeat pounding in her head. And then, as always, the jolt of pain.

Only this was no mending bone, no blinding headache, no aching joint. This was everything and nothing all at once. All colors at once, and yet blackness. All sound at once, and yet silence. All touch at once, and yet emptiness. Through it all, a deep and piercing agony.

Poison. Poison unlike any she'd encountered ran through her veins, and if she didn't dam it up, it'd consume her.

With a gasp, she jolted off the bed. She pressed the heels of her hands to her closed eyes in an attempt to cleanse her mind. The physician said he'd been wounded weeks ago—weeks for the poison to course through his veins, weeks of agony, an unhurried and painful death. This was not the celebrated death a monarch, for all his failings, deserved. This was dark, malevolent, but not the type of unnatural cause Turstin and his fellow physicians had considered.

She lifted her eyes to the fallen king as her heart sunk. The toxin had him in its lethal grasp, and there was nothing she could do for him. Full of weakness, she would not be the author of his fate after all. A wave of relief swept through her. Then the shame.

But neither could she do anything to help him, not when all others' attempts had been futile. If they had found her directly following the accident, she may have held the power to save him. Or she may have condemned him to a slow, miserable death in order to see her own prince ascend the throne, may have proven the lie in her tattoo while proving the truth in her heart. As the sisters had been convinced, the girl whose birth signaled the death of the gift was destined to serve only herself.

Her stomach roiled. The stale chamber was too much for her limited experience with sparring bruises and hunting accidents. Just as she moved toward the window again, the king stirred. Not consciously, not very noticeably, only the movement born of a fever dream. At the foot of the bed, her hands curled around the wooden frame.

Aras shifted restlessly, turning his head from one side to the other. He opened his mouth, his voice so soft that she had to strain to hear it.

"Son. My . . . son."

She straightened. His son was dead and had been for ten years. Men near to death, though, were not bound by time as ordinary men were. Granted the wisdom previously denied them, they reflected on and repented for their errors in time for the Chortove to carry them home to the otherealm.

"I see Turstin's faith in the Order was misplaced," said a silky voice.

A middle-aged man in black physician robes stood just inside the door, hands inside his sleeves. He wore his light-brown hair tied back and his beard neatly clipped. His eyes were a marble blue, steely and unforgiving. If not for the coldness of his gaze, he might have been handsome.

"Excuse me?" she asked, striving for nonchalance as she reached for her dagger behind the cover of her medicine bag. "The Order?"

"Oh, don't play this game," he said. "You're exactly what I think you are—an abomination."

A little flash in her heart said: *Yes, an abomination, indeed. Your birth caused the death of the gift, and the darkness inside you only grows.* Her grip on the dagger handle tightened until her knuckles shone white.

No. Renfred believed in her. That was enough.

The man withdrew his hands from his robes. In one, he held a vial. In the other, a handkerchief.

"What do you want?" she asked, voice rough.

He smiled and rattled the vial. "Do you recognize this? It's naslin."

Her gaze flickered to the fire in the hearth. The bed stood in her way, but she couldn't let him get that vial into the flames, not if she wanted to stay conscious.

"Don't worry," he said. "If you're truly a healer, you would know this won't kill you, merely incapacitate you."

She swallowed thickly. Perhaps if she kept him talking, she could distract him, throw the dagger in his arm or shoulder. "Surely you could arrest me without the help of naslin."

"Why would I arrest you? Oh, you think I want to execute you and claim the bounty for a gifted?" His chuckle sent a shiver through her. "There are those who will reward me quite splendidly for the sale of you."

The *sale* of her?

He held up the naslin. From where he stood, he could throw it straight into the fire.

Turstin reentered. Carrying a basin of water in his arms and a bag of bandages on one shoulder, he paused. The other physician hurriedly stuffed the vial into his pocket.

"Perem," Turstin said with a tense inclination of his head. "I didn't expect you."

"I was merely offering my assistance to our guest," Perem said.

"We've got it well in hand. Thank you." Turstin stepped near the bed and turned toward the door, a clear dismissal.

Perem shot a resentful glare at Aurelia before leaving. Discreetly, she slipped the dagger back into her boot.

"Everything all right?" Turstin asked, setting the basin on a table.

"Yes. Thank you."

"Very well. I can help you apply new dressings."

No need for that now. "Turstin, I'm sorry."

"Please."

"There's nothing I can do for him," she said softly.

He let out a long, slow breath. He closed his eyes and didn't speak for a moment. When finally he opened them, his voice was rough and uneven. "Are you sure?"

She nodded.

"Is it unnatural? Is there someone else we can send for?"

"It's poison," she told him, "but it's like nothing I've ever seen or read about. It's taken root and is attacking his organs. I'm afraid he's beyond help."

"Even yours?"

not strong enough to take this pain from him

"Even mine."

Turstin paled, and his rounded shoulders slumped with the weight of the unwelcome information.

Though she wanted nothing more than to get as far away from this room as possible, to leave this man alone with his grief, she said, "I can treat the wound and prepare an infusion for him to drink thrice a day, but it will give him no more than another few weeks."

His expression was determined. "I don't think you understand the import of this."

Of course she did. She knew exactly how Renfred and the court would react were it Sunniva's queen lying in the place of Temidorus's king. She knew, too, that a poisoned monarch could mean only that a traitor walked free. Turstin's blue eyes widened, as if he were looking for every angle, searching for every possibility, rooting out every lie, even from where he stood. In another life, another time, she would feel bound to help him.

But no matter how ill he was, this man was not her king. Renfred was her prince, her heartfriend, and her sole duty lay in helping him fulfill his destiny.

"I am sorry," she offered quietly.

Such little comfort coming much too late. Turstin remained silent, starting at Aras, whose magnificence was fading out as the flare of a shooting star did—brilliant while it lasted, gone before it could be treasured.

On that childhood day, Aenlic's hilt had shone in the sunlight. People all across Old Inanta—Sunnivan as well as Temidoran—had believed he would be the one destined to raise it to its age of glory. The bright image of that day faded, leaving only a broken man whose sword could not protect him from a silent killer.

The sword.

I am thy downfall.

But if the sword was not Aras's downfall, then what was? Or who?

"Please," said Turstin, placing a hand on her arm, "you mustn't breathe a word of this to anyone."

"You understand he will die, and very soon?"

A mirthless smile crossed the physician's face. "Unfortunately, his death is not my biggest concern at the moment."

"What do you mean?" If it were Renfred on the deathbed, she'd be going mad searching for a way to change his fate.

"The day King Aras renounced the Goddess, he also disbanded his council. He always intended his son to be his heir, and to the day he took the wound, he believed his son could be found."

The sudden conclusion nearly knocked Aurelia to her knees.

Turstin said, "Temidorus has no true sovereign."